THE VIKING GAEL

SAGA

BOOK 1

First paperback edition February 2023
Book design by Nada Orlic

ISBN 978-82-692791-8-4 (paperback)

Published by Old World Heroism, ENK (Norge)
www.oldworldheroism.com

Contents

CHAPTER I   I

CHAPTER II   6

CHAPTER III   11

CHAPTER IV   32

CHAPTER V   42

CHAPTER VI   69

CHAPTER VII   94

CHAPTER VIII 102

CHAPTER IX   123

J.T.T. Ryder

The Viking Gael Saga

"A coward believes he will ever live, if he keep himself safe from strife; but old age leaves him not long in peace, though spears may spare his life."

—Stanza 16 of the Hávamál, from the Poetic Edda.

The Viking Gael Saga

CHAPTER I

The God of Duels

T he two brothers rowed across the bay to duel the old man and his son. Oars pierced through the choppy gray sea and stroked toward the green island. There they would duel two on two, the holmgang.

Four shields and two swords. Four men. One duel.

The small boat hit land and skidded upon the gravelly landing place. The two brothers jumped out and dragged their seacraft up the beach. The younger man carried his older brother's sword, along with their two round, red-painted shields.

That younger man was Asgeir, born of a Norseman from Hordaland and a Gaelic mother from Ireland: "the Viking-Gael," as he would be called by friend and foe alike.

Asgeir looked at his younger brother, Odd, whose wiry veins writhed as he dragged the boat by the bow further up the strand, scraping the loose gravel of the islet. Asgeir handed Odd one shield, who took it by the handle behind its iron boss.

He still held Odd's scabbard in his hands, the oiled leather slick, the brass baldric rattling as they walked over the strand. The sword called Gael-Kisser. The pride of their father, who warrior-walked as huskarl of the King of Lothlend. A fine-crafted weapon—their father always said that if the dwarves had ever banged out a nail, they surely had smithed Gael-Kisser.

The blade, reforged with a splinter of the skull of their ancestor, rasped as Odd drew it from the scabbard. The wool fleece inside kept it well-oiled;

a man who brings a rusty weapon to a duel would affront Ullr, god of dueling. The sun lit the sword through the overcast sky. Gray sword, gray ocean, gray sky.

In the middle of the island, an old man with a scarred face tightened the belt around his chainmail. He unsheathed his sword and pointed it at the brothers. A younger man stood near him, wearing the same face as the drawn, scarred old man, just smooth. They bore two round shields, spiraled in yellow and white.

Ulf the Old grinned, and the lines deepened on his cheeks. His son, Rolf Ulfsson, stood by his side, shielded.

The two brothers eyed the father and son. The foamy waves crashed on the beach and soaked up the younger brother's gray winingas that wrapped his legs from foot to knee.

Their enemies stood near the ring of hazel rods. The battlefield. The dueling square. Where men stood athwart another, where honor brandished, where men inveighed against their cowardice. Asgeir awaited the holmgang on the gray island, under the gray sky, against his gray-mailed enemy.

Asgeir looked back toward his farm on the misty hillside across the bay. He shivered and sweated as gulls screeched overhead. The chimney puffed out thick billows of smoke.

Odd bit his upper lip until blood dribbled down his cleft chin.

Ulf sheathed his sword, set his shield facedown with the leather strap wound up, and unhooked the bronze buckle of his belt. He stooped over and wiggled his body until his chainmail shimmied off him in a pile. He righted the madder-dyed hat on his head, belted himself around his weld-dyed tunic, seized his shield and unsheathed his sword.

"Ullr blesses those who fight with honor, and that is I, Ulf the Old," he said and stepped over the circle's threshold. Rolf followed him in.

"The gods love youthful men, and laugh at elderly men that have lived as long as you," Odd said. "Your chance to forfeit still stands. Return to the hearth to speak your old tales to your grandchildren, and let this folly end. We won't be sailors on your ship. I don't care what debt our father owes you. Flee from this duel, and we will return to our farm."

"You talk too long. Swords speak quickly."

Odd, with a smile, bent his knees down. With one leap, he cleared the hazel rod border in a man's length and landed in a crouch. He sprang back up. As Asgeir crossed the threshold, the scent of his sweaty brother tinged the breeze.

His brother had the wild about him, sure-footed, cord-muscled, youthful. Ulf the Old, his thin gray hair fluttering in the wind from under his close-fitting hat, took a long sigh, and his joints creaked as he leaned about to stretch.

Ulf and Odd approached each other, swords drawn, until they remained just outside sword's reach. Their blade tips were poised at each other's chests. Their shield-bearers, Rolf and Asgeir, stood beside the swordsmen. Rolf put a hand on his father's shoulder and kept it there. Asgeir placed his own hand on Odd's stiff, hard arm.

"Take your hand off me," Odd said, "you don't need to follow my lead. I'm nimbler than that geezer."

Asgeir pulled away, but still stood a pace from his brother. They all planted their feet on the ground. The circle hemmed in around Asgeir, as if the hazel rods had shrunk.

"Last chance, old man," Odd said with a laugh.

"I'll send you laughing to the ground."

The points of the two swords touched and, with a scrape, the god Ullr commanded them to do him honor.

Odd struck at Ulf, spittle flying from his thin lips. Ulf spun his shield up, and Gael-Kisser clanged off the iron boss. The old man arced and thrust at Odd, but Asgeir blocked the blow for his brother.

Blade against blade, Ulf and Odd rang and rasped. Odd freed his sword from a parry by Ulf and, with a sidestep, stabbed at the throat of his enemy, but Rolf's shield slapped the sword away from his father.

Ulf flipped his shield over his arm and turned his wrist as he jumped forward with a stab. Asgeir raised his shield but found himself too far away. Odd had lunged forward, his shield too low, his sword poised to strike the leg of his enemy. There was a gurgle. The tip of Ulf's sword had plunged into Odd's eye.

Asgeir blanched as Odd crumbled to his knees. His brother's shield fell from his hand, rolled a span on its rawhide brim, and rumbled to the soggy ground. Ulf placed a foot on Odd's quaking chest and yanked the sword free. A spout of blood. Red brains on the gray blade pointed to the gray heavens.

A pair of oystercatchers flew up from a cove nearby. Their white-black fat bodies flitted as they soared above the surf. They flew westward over the sea.

"He talked too much," Ulf said to his son with a heave of breath. "I'm old, but my sword sings on note," he stopped to cough, "just as when I had the body of Freyr."

"Pappa, we won," Rolf said as Odd sprawled out on his back, shivering in death-throes.

"I didn't mean to kill him," Ulf said, "but arrogance has taken its toll."

Odd wiggled, Gael-Kisser still in his bluing hand. Ulf stooped over and pried each finger from the leathered grip of the sword. He ran his own finger down the silver wires twisted into the grooves of the steel pommel.

"Gael-Kisser. The sword of the first king of Lothlend," Ulf said as he placed his finger on the blade near the pommel and lifted it aloft, "the blade to first fell an Irish king."

Asgeir dragged Odd's shield close to his corpse and pulled his dead brother upon its underside. His glassy, unblinking eye stared into nothing as his mouth drooled blood. The red jelly that was once his eye had splattered over his face in mince.

Odd, Asgeir thought, *your eyes and father's were so alike. Why'd you go and get killed? Who's going to take care of the farm over winter? Poor Mamma... I won't even be around when he's buried.*

"This will be your sword after I settle the deal with your father," Ulf said to Asgeir. "Now go home and fetch your things. We leave at daybreak."

Asgeir sat wordless next to his dead brother.

"Summer has come and nearly gone, so we must begin our voyage now," Ulf said. "Your brother lost. Your family will grieve and bury him, and you may visit his grave when you return someday. Now go on, bring him back to your mother. Stuff something in your ears before she goes screeching."

Nothing. Just gray sky, gray island, one gray brother.

Something wet. Something dripped. The flat of Ulf's bloody blade on Asgeir's head.

"Your brother agreed to duel, if you lost, you would serve as my deckhands, and I won."

Asgeir scuttled away from Ulf with lowered eyes, little red rubies of blood speckled on his face.

"Fear me if you may," Ulf said, "but under my wing, you'll be a Viking-Gael just as your father."

Asgeir knelt down by his brother and, with a retch, slung him over his shoulders. He heaved up to his feet and trudged back to the boat. He placed his warm, graying brother into the hull and leaned him against the bench. Someone shadowed him, and he found Rolf there, holding two red-faced shields, Asgeir's and Odd's.

Asgeir placed the shields into the flat bottom. He pushed the stern and sloshed through the cold seawater which seeped up into his winingas, and boarded the boat. With one oar, he shoved seaward, but after nine strokes, he looked back to the island. Ulf and his son stood with chins skyward. Praying to Ullr, god of duels.

The bolts of Odd's shield rattled as the waves hit the boat.

"I won't fight under that captain with the same shield as you, brother. For Odd. An honorable death."

He flung his own shield out of the boat. It wheeled along the surface of the water and sank. Just one rower in the boat now, he stroked back landward, homeward, brotherless, shieldless, and soon, homeless.

Ulf the Old had won the duel, and Asgeir would follow the oystercatchers westward over the sea, just two black pins against the gray sky over the horizon. Westward, would they fly to Hjaltland? From there, where? To the Faroes, or Iceland, or could their flight take them to the lands of the Viking-Gaels, where he had been born? Ulf yearned to raid again, this time down in Ireland, and would now drag Asgeir along as a deckhand.

I'll avenge you, Odd.

CHAPTER II

The Curse

Abane upon your ship," Auntie Bjorg said as the yellow-clad men hauled their stuffs onto the beached ship. She wore a moss-green dress trimmed in beaver fur, with twin silvered brooches above her breasts that glinted in the dim light. She was sixty winters old with gray hair like silk threads. She vanished into the gloom of their house upon the hill.

Asgeir and his mother, Frainche, embraced at their farm's landing place. She wore a tear-stained, weld-dyed robe cinched at the waist by a green cord. He looked down at his little sister, Hildr, who hugged his leg, her stringy blond hair askew over her ashen face.

Ulf stood upon the deck of his longship, a drakkar, with his son Rolf at his side. The forty-nine-foot seacraft had been dragged up the landing place of the Damsgaard farm, Asgeir's home. A train of eighteen men swung sacks of wheat, rye, oats, and barley over its gunwale, where a handful of thralls, recognizable by their undyed tunics and grim demeanors, worked to fit the freight below deck. Their crew lacked numbers, and Asgeir knew Ulf needed men—oarsmen, deckhands, spearmen—for his raid in Ireland.

And the sailors he has now know his thews are strong enough to lead such a crew of vikings.

"Leave some space for plunder, by the gods!" a short sailor said as the thralls toiled. He was Njall Gray-Hair, first mate of Ulf's crew.

Auntie Bjorg bore a long iron distaff with a bulbous wrought-iron head. The staff of the völva, a seeress who unraveled the fates of men, if they dared know their own fates. She waved it as if to etch something vile upon the ship's port side.

"You shall wreck," she said. The gruff-looking men of the baggage train slowed, and one sailor frowned as the sack he carried slipped from his hands.

"In the realm of Ran you will dwell," she said. "I call the west wind's storm against your journey. Many will drown. And you, Ulf," she poised the staff at him, "will never know peace in your old age, for you will face a fate worse than a drowned man. Misfortune will befall you, all but my nephew, Asgeir, who will survive with my brother's sword in his hand."

A trio of Ulf's men grumbled.

"To the sea with your spite, witch," Ulf said. "Your brother owes me deckhands, and I'm taking one now. Winter is upon us, and I won't wait another season for this voyage."

"Just do as he says. Thor will protect you, and your afterbirth spirit— your fylgja—guides you," Frainche said with her arms hugged around Asgeir's shoulders. Her hot tears trickled down his neck and her blond plait swatted about as she hugged him tight.

I hate how I can do nothing while my mother cries.

"You're not meant to go a'viking. You're the son who will inherit the farm. He can't take you," she said. The wetness of her face tasted salty to Asgeir.

"I will," Ulf said.

"I'll miss you," she said in Gaelic.

"I'll miss you both, but I'll return from Ireland someday," he said back in Gaelic. He cradled both his mother and sister.

Asgeir looked back to his farm. Smoke billowed from the chimney of his boat-shaped house on the hillock, its open doorway aglow from the hearth inside. One he-thrall in the garden near the house with the onions, carrots, and cabbage. A she-thrall up with the sheep in the hills. Seven more he-thralls toiling about the fields before the last harvest of the year. The thralls that hauled boats over the isthmus and had been born over on the South Islands. Or Ireland. Did thralls from Hordaland toil on Irish land?

The last of the hemp sacks were passed across the train, and all had been loaded in the cargo hold. Ulf's sailors marched up the gangway of the ship.

"The sail is set, the course is laid, the first journey of the late year! Ho!"

Two of Ulf's youths, one round-faced and black-haired, the other blond and thewy, swung their legs over the gunwale and dropped to the deck.

Asgeir looked down at his mother. She cursed in Gaelic under her breath.

"Let me go, mamma. I'll row with them, and that'll give me passage to Lothlend, where I will find pappa. He's a huskarl to the King, so he will set this all right. Just because we haven't heard word from him since the summer doesn't mean he's hurt or in danger. And Ulf has Gael-Kisser, and it belongs to us."

"They're taking you so far away," she replied. "They're taking you to Ireland."

"I know, but the sword belongs to us. And I want to see my father."

"Your father hadn't returned," she said, and peered over his head and squinted her eyes at the two youths.

The youths gasped and halted working as Bjorg chanted with her raspy voice:

> To Ran with your ship,
> A hex from my lip,
> The waves I shall lead,
> In the great gray mead.

Some of the sailors peeked their heads over the rail; one shuddered. Ulf propped himself up behind them on a pair of long chests and ruffled the hair of the two sailors.

"Let the snake spew her venom, the bitter, childless crone she is. We sacrificed to Njordr, who protects travelers, and so shall we come to land again. And quit your crying, Frainche, your boy will return someday," he said, and gestured toward Asgeir. "Now come on, lad! We sail past the isle of Eigg—your old home. We'll rest there for a night, I am sure you miss it."

"I don't," Asgeir said.

I may have been born on that little island, but my family is here. Pappa, I'll find you, but I will return back to Norway.

"I love you, and so do the gods," Frainche said in Gaelic as she kissed her son on both cheeks.

"I will return, mamma, and with father," he said, and looked at the red-leather baldric of Ulf. And the sword shall hang from my shoulder, he thought, and pried himself from his mother's grasp.

A cat crested a hillock with a mouse dangling from its mouth, and the sailors laughed at the sight. It crossed the stone-paved path to Asgeir's home, pranced up to him, and let the mouse loose. The mouse stood still on its hindlegs, shivering. The fluffy black cat switched its tail and cooed.

The two youths laughed as they walked toward Asgeir. "Good little hunter," one said.

"Ah, a mouser!" Ulf said, "and just in time. And you idiots think ill luck will strike us? A fair sign from Freya herself. Take it!"

Asgeir yelped to spook the cat, it pivoted, but the black-haired youth pinched the scruff of the cat as it darted past his foot.

"This is his home!" Asgeir said. "It's not right for you to take him."

The blond youth stomped his leather boot down upon the mouse and pulled his foot back up; half the red mouse stuck to it. He stripped it off and boarded the ship.

Ulf, standing near the rudder, petted the cat. "His name is Svartganger."

"Our farm needs him," Asgeir said. "There will be more mice come winter."

"Svartganger the Lucky," Ulf said. "You hear that, you sea-wolves? We have a lucky cat, so forget the völva's ravings." The cat lay upon a chest with the half-mouse twixt its paws and chewed on it.

At least I'll have some company on the ship.

"A pox on your voyage!" Bjorg cried, and pointed a catskin-gloved finger at Ulf. The glove of the völva, the power of Freya, goddess of cats, who the seeress drew upon for spells.

Ulf jutted his lower jaw out as the sailors looking on from the ship halted again. One grumbled.

"And if not," Ulf said, "we'll skin him and make the witch a second glove." He went astarboard.

Asgeir walked up the ramp, the planks rumbling underfoot, and he found a well-stocked ship with many sailors preparing for the voyage. He turned back at his mother, who was cuddling his little teary sister, and they both watched wordless. The wind whipped their hair across their faces.

The sail was hoisted, the ship's hold full of things, the chests placed under the rowlocks. Each sailor sat and grabbed an oar that cranked in its socket.

The wind blew southeasterly across the gray sea.

"Off to the kaupaungr to stock up on supplies," Ulf said, "and when we return home from Ireland, our sail shall be red as blood."

Asgeir sat upon a three-legged stool and held the oar in his hands. Its blade had been sanded fine, but veined green by algae. The sailors sat upon chests along both rails of the ship, some shut with iron locks. Ulf's chest sat at the back, near the rudder. Gael-Kisser lay there.

The Damsgaard thralls pushed at the prow of the boat, knee-deep in the sea as the men on the starboard side rowed. The ship swerved alongside the shore, the surf raised the hull, and the portside oarsmen now rowed.

Asgeir sat on a stool near the rudder, and he looked backward once more. His mother and sister looked on from the grassy shore. Their herd dog guarded the sheep and cows that grazed in the uplands.

Farewell, Damsgaard. His eyes nearly welled up when he found his mother and Hildr at the shoreline, watching as the ship drew further from them. I'll miss you, but I'll return.

Just ahead, the gray mist of the distance. Gray sky. Gray sea. Gray seal in a pool nearby. It dunked into the water and never came back up. All the while, Bjorg chanted downwind:

> *To Ran with your ship,*
>
> *A hex from my lip,*
>
> *The waves I shall lead,*
>
> *In the great gray mead.*

Svartganger the Lucky crunched up his mouse until nothing but slivers of red lay flecked about the deck, and stalked down into the innards of the ship. Asgeir shimmied the oar along with the other sailors, all strangers to him. None of them said a word as the range between his family and the ship stretched. The wind blew bitter against his face.

Ulf, steering the rudder, shouted, "To the kaupaungr!"

The ship sailed northward over the calm fjord as Damsgaard melded into the distant, cloudless gloom.

CHAPTER III

The Raid

Asgeir rowed with Ulf and his vikings in midafternoon up the fjord. As the drakkar, called the Sea-Bitch, glided over the soft blue sea, wall-like mountains on either side stretched higher and blotted out the sun. The fjord ended at a greensward nestled in the dale where a river ran inland. At the gravelly landing place, a figure with a red cloak flitting behind him put a foot on a mooring-stone and placed a hand on the bronze hilt of his sheathed sword. Fifty paces behind him, a camp garrisoned by shirtless warriors, armed with spears, stood by a moored longship.

"You must pay the landing fee to me, the huskarl Ketill Redcloak, captain of the longship Head-Charger, in the name of Jarl Haakon of Borgund," he said. He stood in the shadow cast by the mountains. The ship eased closer, and the bow scraped the fjord bed.

The man looked young, with a curled mustache. Besides his cloak and sword-belt, his clothes appeared simple—green needlebound hat, brown and green tunic, hose, and winingas. His shoes were ragged and in need of waxing. A blond-maned horse grazed, hitched to a fence.

"A landing-fee at the river mouth," Ulf said, "and maybe another downriver, before the market. Then another at the market."

"You can pay whinging or you can pay silently."

Ulf grumbled as the sailors hauled out a sack from the ship and dragged it ashore to the young man. Asgeir had heard of him, because he had sworn fealty to the Jarl of Laerdal. The jarls, the rulers-by-blood, descended from Odin and walked Midgard as leaders and priests, only overshadowed by kings. His father had been a jarl before he had voyaged to the lands of the Gaels, before Frainche birthed Asgeir.

"That's all," Ketill said, and toyed with a strand of his mustache. "There are some Finnmen at the market. Catch them if you would like their wares. Reindeer antlers, ropes, tar…"

Ulf said nothing as he and his men pushed the ship back out into the waves. The sailors hoisted the sail, the wind caught it, and they floated upriver and sailed into the valley called Laerdal.

"There's no more honor," Ulf said. "The jarls shear us until our hides raw. And if you disagree, they silence you; if you keep speaking, they send you to the gallows." He removed his hat, and his sparse long hair fluttered in the wind.

"Nowadays, a man's son is less honorable than he," Ulf said. "They believe they have the right to take food from travelers, rather than give them food as guests. Neighbors and kinsmen turn into thieves."

The undercurrent rapped hard against the ship, and the sailors plashed against it. Asgeir's stool rumbled under him as the rapids pummeled the hull. In the distance, a long waterfall poured, a giant's free-fall.

"Few agree to duels, even, where honor shines like starlight against this grim world. Yes, few have honor. Your brother had honor," Ulf said to Asgeir as he steered the ship around the bend, "but he was young. He had the youthful zest about him. Good to be zesty, until it gets you killed. But he died with honor."

Asgeir's hands gripped his oar hard as he turned from Ulf's steely gaze. He rowed hard upstream.

"Yet your family was awfully sour."

"They needed me over winter," Asgeir said. "Until my father returns, I'm the last man at Damsgaard."

"Man?" Ulf said, and smirked. "You're no man yet. But the sea will make you one, when we sail over to Hjaltland and round Cape Wrath. Maybe you'll be a man then, yes, when Njordr, the god of the seas, drenches you and freezes you and offers you no kindness."

This man will kill you someday, Ulf, or die in honor.

They passed farmstead after farmstead, which were bordered by long walls, fences, or streams. A distant din as loud as a thousand horses in gallop poured from upriver. Smoke billowed up from the trees that bearded the mountain. A rumble quaked through the valley, swift, sudden, and then silent. A woman arose from a garden near a small longhouse, and pointed upriver.

"Rockslide!" she called to the ship. Her linen wimple flapped in the wind. Ulf huffed. "Press on."

The ship rounded the bend, breeze in the sail. A rockfall cluttered the riverway several spans away from the ship.

"Halt!" someone shouted as the sailors rowed astern to stop the ship.

A boulder stuck out of the river like a peened bolt. More boulders likely lurked just under the surface.

"The trolls," a sailor said. "That's what they say about landslides here. It's an ill sign."

"Just what I needed—shall I pay the fucking trolls a tax, too?" Ulf said, and snorted. "Come on, you idiots, drop anchor—we don't want to scrape the hull over that thing or drag the keel over any jagged rocks—and out of the ship—move out!"

The first mate lobbed the iron anchor overboard, and it struck the riverbed. Next came the rope ladder, which unfurled over the side of the boat, but a woman's yell flew upriver.

"It's too dangerous," the woman with the wimple said. She came riverward and stood on the soft turf of the bank. She looked about forty winters, clad in a whitish-red dress. "The current is strong because of last week's heavy rain. It will wash you lot back down to Ran."

Ulf shouted at the woman, "I'll hear none of Ran!"

The woman shirked away but then righted her feet. "I apologize."

"I suppose we'll wait for low tide. Your warning is heeded," Ulf said, and strummed his fingers along the rail.

"I'm Gro of Rocky Bend, and you're welcome to warm your cold hide in my home," she said with a smile. She gestured toward a longhouse a few hundred paces from the riverside. "The folks of Laerdal would never turn away guests in need."

"Bold of a woman to invite a gaggle of sailors into her home," Ulf said.

"Even bolder to think the lawman wouldn't hear of misbehaving guests," Gro said.

Drifting down the bend, a smaller ship swayed up the river, rowed by two dozen hardy men. A man clad in red walked through the sweaty sailors, the crew of the Head-Charger. Ketill's men raised their oars and rowed astern until their boats drifted broadside toward the Sea-Bitch, but slowed and stopped just a plank away. An anchor plunged through the water.

"Ho, men!" Ketill hailed the sailors of the Sea-Bitch. "Ill luck has struck us both. Perhaps the trolls dislike us equally. Let us work together."

"I think it's best to wait until low tide," Ulf said, "and we've been invited to be guests in this lady's home."

"It was I who told you to wait until low tide," she said, "but the more the merrier. Come on the lot of you, then."

The sailors rowed their ships portside toward the bank and started climbing down, landing on the soft turf, starting up through the reeds of the outfield.

Ulf stayed put, and when Asgeir walked past, the old man grabbed him by the shoulder and yanked him back.

"Nope, not you, boy," he said. "You stay on board, and so do I. Someone's guarding the ship."

I'll follow orders, and bide my time.

The old captain whistled at the last three men disembarking the ship. "And you boys—sit your asses down."

A woman emerged from behind Ketill's sailors, her hair in plaits and capped in a linen headscarf. She wore two oval-shaped bronze brooches at each strap of the flame-colored apron-dress that marked her as a landed, married lady. The brooches glowed in the sun as she climbed over the rail, her red-nailed hands unsteady on the ladder.

Ulf clicked his tongue at the sight of the woman, halting his descent down the ladder. The woman in turn laid a hand over her own mouth when she sighted him.

"I think the old man is afraid to climb down the ladder," Ketill said.

"I think that young men with tongues such as yours do not live to be old men," Ulf said. "And I think this she-wolf has smelled fresh meat—does her husband know you hold her hand?"

Ketill frowned as the lady, red-faced, climbed down the ladder. She met Gro, and they embraced with wide smiles.

"These strangers may be up to no good, the old man has much to prove—go on, guard dogs against this gray fox," Ketill said to his men. Gro hugged his arm as they, along with the lady and a cohort of men, walked up toward the farmhouse.

"The she-wolf has her fangs in his balls," Ulf said to his men. "Who knows what lies she is slobbering in his ear. She's still sore about her husband, that bone-faced dishonorable Rudolf High-Hat, outlawed to the Orkneys."

Four men remained on the deck of Ketill's ship, gruff, as the rest of the crews trekked up the tawny outfield, across the green fields, and into the white-painted longhouse from which the breeze brought the scent of stew back to the ships.

Svartganger caressed himself between Asgeir's ankles. Asgeir leaned down to pet the cat, who purred, but cast a round-eyed glance over at the crew of the Head-charger.

Just what did we get caught up in, Svartganger?

After a spell, Ulf and his men dragged their chests into a circle, gestured for the other crew to come aboard their ship and cast their bone dice.

Ketill's men boarded the Sea-Bitch, the circle widened, and gusty laughter peeled up from the deck as the two crews wagered their dice. Asgeir sat on his stool away from them, Svartganger trilling on his lap and kneading his tunic, but a hard laugh from a sailor after a click of the dice startled the cat, and he scurried away.

The cold breeze in the hot sun brought the scent of stew to Asgeir. His belly churned. He lifted up the lid of his basket and took out some dried pork. As he chewed, he heard something rustling.

Is that my afterbirth spirit? My fylgja? That mamma said would guide me? The red fur of a fox flitted among some blackberry bushes. He stole over to the railing and placed a foot on it, but Ulf's voice cut him.

"Where are you going, boy?" Ulf asked as he cast a die, then muttered under his breath.

"To piss," Asgeir said.

"Not big enough to aim it over the rail?" said one of Ulf's sailors, named Erle, who had a salty red beard. They all laughed.

"I may have to shit also."

"Well then go on, find some bushes," Ulf said as he slapped the side of the ship. "She doesn't need another paint job."

Asgeir climbed down the ladder, landed on the soggy ground, and parted the undergrowth. He caught Ulf eying him over the rail, so he squatted in the bushes. After Ulf's head vanished back into the ship, he crawled through the bushes. Pricked by thorns, and with the jerky still between his teeth, he went off to find the fox.

I need to get away from those vikings, even just for a little while. Maybe I can escape and be as free as that fox. To Ran with Ulf and his stinking crew!

Dancing around the clumpy plowed field, the white-breasted kit sniffed and hid. Asgeir broke off a chunk of pork and tossed it to him. The fox sniffed, nosed it around in the dirt, snatched it, and swallowed it.

"Nosey," Asgeir said, "that's your name."

Asgeir threw some more morsels until the kit had eaten half his jerky.

The beast scampered away uphill. The tramp of the two crews downhill through the trackway of the farm had scared it away. Some thralls came down from the wooded hill behind the house, leading an ox. A woman's red-nailed, bony hand pulled the door shut behind the last man to leave.

Asgeir hid among the bushes until they passed. He found Nosey up by a drystone wall near the longhouse.

One more bite for him. The longer I'm away from that ship, the better, but I suppose I need to get back. No sense in running away now.

Asgeir stooped down and ran up the hill while Nosey pranced about the eastern gable of the house. He approached gingerly, his hand outstretched toward the sniffing fox. The fox crept forward, snatched the meat out of his hand, and bounded away. At the river, the thralls led the ox down into the river. As Asgeir left, voices rose from the other, mountain-facing ingang of the house.

"The old man is a dead man," a woman's voice said in Norse, but with a twang Asgeir had not heard before. He slunk against the longhouse and cupped his ear toward their voices. "My husband would rather slay himself than allow that old man to live. Now is our chance for revenge."

"He is so insulting—just who does he think he is?" said another woman, who Asgeir recognized as Gro.

"He's the bastard son of a jarl, that's who. He lived an idle life. Now he's decrepit, he goes a'viking," the other woman said.

"Ketill should duel him. The old goat would stand no chance against the jarl's ram," Gro said.

"He doesn't deserve a duel—we'll take care of him."

"What are you thinking?"

"At the marketplace, we'll insist that he meet us. His wife died years ago, so he must be lonely—one of us will have a beautiful maiden that we may be interested in marrying to him. His crew should be heading to Hjaltland before winter. We'll invite him back here for some drinks the night before he leaves. He'll trust us—who would ever poison a guest? And he won't survive the night!"

Gro gasped.

"Don't you act surprised—he insulted you, too, Gro. You told me how he shouted at you just for warning him of the rockslide—that is what kind of man he is."

"We may affront Odin," Gro said. "We can't just poison a guest! Not in my home!"

"And who has that dotard not affronted? He insulted me while my husband is in Orkney and my son is up hunting in the mountains! No one can even defend my honor! And you know what he did to my husband and I, years ago."

"I forbid this to take place in my house," Gro said. "Poison a guest in your own house."

"It's best if we lure him to Ketill's hall in Rikheim. Ketill will be much displeased to learn it was Ulf that had a hand in wronging my husband. Ketill and he were friends before that unjust decree of outlawry for my Rudolf... yes, and Ketill keeps a lovely hall. I'll even send for my daughter."

"I won't chirp," Gro said, "and no one knows I grow nightshade in my garden. Sure, he deserves it, but I don't want that stain on my door."

"He's a stain," the other woman said with a growl. "A stain we should dab clean."

"Then we should meet him at the market."

Asgeir wrung his hands. *Murder? Poison? Maybe Ulf is right and people have no honor nowadays...*

He walked back riverward.

Even he doesn't deserve to die like that.

Stooping down through the bushes, he found the ox knee-deep in the river, crowded by shirtless men. The beast had been yoked to the boulder and, with the crews of both the Sea-Bitch and the Head-Charger, started to drag the boulder toward the eastern side of the river by many ropes.

Maybe I shouldn't say a word—and let the Norns decide if he dies like a coward. But would that be honorable?

He slew my brother in a fair fight—I should be the one to slay him, not nightshade!

Beast and man moved the boulder, and the sailors heaved and huffed as they pulled the smaller rocks out of the waterway. Ulf left the pull-gang when he spotted Asgeir and marched through the water toward him. He snatched a short length of rope up from the ground, and red-faced, snapped it between his hands.

"You weren't just taking a shit," Ulf said.

Asgeir swallowed the half-chewed pork hard. Ulf snapped the rope again.

"How many lashes do you deserve?"

"Ulf!"

"Just what were you doing?" he took a step closer, and Asgeir felt the river-stench about him.

Many of Ketill's crewmen lurked about; Ketill himself led the ox ashore and back on the trackway where the thralls of the house had massed.

"I can't tell you now," Asgeir said in an undertone. Some stragglers from the Head-Charger crew still lingered in earshot. "But I have a good reason."

Ulf snapped the whip right into Asgeir's eye. The world flashed white as Asgeir found himself ass-first on the ground. Ulf had already started back to the ship. The skin around his eye ached. *If my father had seen him do that to me... that bastard.*

Perhaps I should just let those witches poison him.

At high tide, the keels of the ships raised off the riverbed, and both ships rowed upriver.

The Sea-Bitch sailed through Laerdal. Asgeir's one good eye lay on the green mountains shrouded in mist. They passed the meeting of three valleys, where the farm of Rikheim lay. The Head-Charger veered off the riverway homeward, while the Sea-Bitch headed east to Bjorkum, the kaupaungr. Further downstream, a tor shaped like a troll couple with a baby stood bestride a waterfall. The craggy family marked the place of the kaupaungr, and all knew to head trollward to find it.

He gazed at the trolls. Once when Odin had traveled the dale, his horse had an itch. The horse scratched its ass against a rock. The troll couple laughed at his mount, so Odin turned them into rocks. Afterward, they guarded the kaupaungr from insulting and rude guests, dishonest merchants, and raids.

He stared at Ulf, hand on the rudder. The gods had been on Asgeir's side, for he hadn't been blinded when Ulf's rope smote him.

"So tell me, you rascal," Ulf said with a grin, "why you disobeyed me?"

"It doesn't matter why," Asgeir said, "but now I can tell you, even though I have half a mind not to."

"Oh?"

"My honor demands I do," Asgeir said, and Ulf's face relaxed.

"Go on."

"Ketill and that housewife your crew stayed with are plotting to murder you."

Ulf's hand pushed hard on the rudder as the ship drifted shoreward, but he righted it.

"I knew that harlot was spinning treachery," he said.

"They will meet you at the market," Asgeir said. "They'll invite you to Rikheim, where you'll be poisoned at dinner."

"Is that so?" Ulf said as his grin widened wolfishly. The wind stilled as he looked over his shoulder back at Rikheim just as it vanished around the oxbow. "You overheard this?"

"Yes—Gro and another woman were speaking as you were dragging the rocks out of the river."

"I almost regret that I whipped you," Ulf said. "You have no love for me—why tell me? How do I know you aren't trying to trick me?"

"I'd rather see you die with honor than murdered."

He killed Odd, and whipped me. Asgeir blinked the wetness away. *But it was a duel. Ulf wouldn't have just poisoned him. Once my father learns of this, we will settle this legally. Until then, I will wait, and keep him alive. I'll save his life now, so someday it will be me standing over his dying body in Ullr's circle.*

"And you will save that honor for yourself?" he said, and winked at the lad.

Ulf and Asgeir eyed each other, but Asgeir broke the stare-down first, turning to row.

"What age is this, the age of the weasel?" Ulf said. "The wren? The cockroach? Our ancestors lived through the age of gold, the wolf, the bear." His voice raised louder, and he shouted downwind. "Treachery is afoot, men! We may be the last warriors in an age of cowards! They insult their elders, they tax every span you travel for every length of their cocks, and lowly trollish bitches conspire behind the back of men to murder a warrior! And who will accept this? Not I!"

The sailors shouted back, "Not I!" Asgeir stayed silent.

"We go onward to the kaupaungr," Ulf said as he seized a spear and slammed the iron ferrule against the deck. "We stock up. We get our tar, our lanolin, our stockfish. We prepare for our journey to Hjaltland—but first, we stock up on the spoils of Rikheim!"

The sailors all cheered, and Ulf cheered louder over them, until their cheering sank into a wordless song as they turned the ship. The troll family grew smaller and grayer and dimmer, the river narrower, and the white tents of the kaupaungr fell out of view.

Asgeir clenched his teeth. *If Ulf is killed in this raid, then I won't have my revenge. But what if I die in this raid? This isn't my fight.* He plashed the oar blade into the water as it trembled in his hands. Soon, the grassy roof of Rikheim came into view.

The farm of Rikheim stood upon high, flat land, where a steep slope ran down to the landing place on the riverside. A boathouse stood there, and the Sea-Bitch had been dragged up the muddy shore next to it. The crew furled up the sail and left their oars in their rowlocks as they armed themselves with spears. A sailor snatched the shield off the gunwale next to Asgeir.

A raid already, and in Norway at that. The lawman won't like this. I was hoping to avoid war. I've never been in a battle– by Thor!

The spears gleamed in the sun as the vikings poured out of the ship one by one. Asgeir caught sight of one spearpoint that was burnished to a mirror-shine.

Thor, defend me—may I live to see another day, so I may fight and kill Ulf.

Ulf clad himself in his chainmail with the help of a thrall, and another thrall belted Gael-Kisser in its scabbard around his waist.

"Odin, the Lord of Spears, calls me," Ulf said. "I lived too long, and now I have seen an age of dishonor. Well, I'll have none of it! Will you?"

"No!" the sailors shouted, except Asgeir.

A horn blared in the distance and echoed throughout the three valleys. Asgeir spotted three small boats rowing hard from further down the river toward Rikheim.

"Come on, you half-starved sea-wolves!" Ulf shouted. He unsheathed the sword, hopped off the gunwale, and landed on his feet despite his age. "You've been slacking! The day is young and wanting of blood!"

The sailors all raised their white-yellow shields to their bodies as they disembarked.

"Stay here," Njall said to Asgeir. "Go hide in that noost, but keep watch, don't just play with your cock while we're gone."

They hurried up the hill from the landing place to Rikheim. The hall stretched as long as a ship with a turfed-over roof. A goat munched on grass from the roof, and two he-thralls fled from the sheds into the hills. Some men funneled into the house from the rear entrance, spearpoints gleaming in the sun. Asgeir found some hewn stone blocks near the boathouse and sneaked toward them.

Thank Thor, I can hide at least.

The boathouse, also with a turfed roof and a stone-built foundation, had a boat docked inside. Asgeir climbed up the algae-covered wall of the noost, then hid himself in a nook in the drystone.

The goat hopped off the hall roof and pranced off into the distance as one more young man dashed into the house, dragging a two-handed spear. Someone from inside shut the door.

"Enemy spearmen!" Ulf shouted. "They've grown some balls then. Two of you," he said to Njall and another, shorter sailor, "in front! The rest of you, stab over their heads!"

Ulf, spear in one hand and shield in the other, kicked the door down in one hard burst. It fell inward, and then javelins flew outward in a rain of iron. Ulf raised his shield to defend himself, as did many of the men, but one of his sailors crumpled to the sward with a javelin-point lodged in his throat. He groaned, and blood drained and reddened the grass as the sailors stepped over him.

Asgeir found himself breathless.

More dead for Ulf! Poor Odd, you died even more suddenly…

"Won't be an easy raid," Ulf said. "Good, Odin loves the bold!"

Asgeir peered over some loose walling. The two shorter men raised their shields over their heads as they advanced on the house. They stabbed with their spears through the doorway, over the fallen, cracked wooden door.

Inside, the hearth cast red light upon the defenders as they struck with their spears against the invaders. Outside, the attackers hurled spears through the doorway over the ground awash in blood.

"Greetings, child," a whispery voice said from the river.

Asgeir bolted at the sound and reached for a weapon, but he found a girl swimming with just her chin above the surface. She had red hair tangled over her face like kelp. She must have been his age.

"Who are you?"

"A mermaid," the girl said, expressionless. She had big green eyes, and a splash of freckles browned her face.

"You're a girl," Asgeir said.

Have I been struck silly by Ulf's whip? There's a battle going on, and she's just swimming in that cold water. She can't really be a mermaid, can she?

"Are mermaids not girls?"

"You're just a girl. Isn't it cold?"

"I do not shiver," she said, but her white lips belied her state, "for I am a mermaid, a daughter of Ran. Your people make much evil against this farm. They feed me fish, so I like them, and I bring them luck. You've angered me!"

"They aren't my people," Asgeir said.

Just over the hewn blocks stacked near the boathouse, a splintered spearshaft shot through the air.

"I'll bring you bad luck now," she said.

Her shout of the foulest, most baleful word echoed almost as loud as the battle-sounds clanked.

"You're just a girl out for a swim, and I ought to be keeping watch," he said as he huddled against the wall, worried about wayward darts.

"I am a daughter of Ran," she said. She squinted her eyes and shook her head to throw her hair over her lithesome shoulders.

"Then prove it, show me your flippers."

The girl raised herself out of the fjord, and streamlets flowed down her breasts, just visible under her hemp dress. She lunged backward into the sea and then emerged again.

"Follow me," she said, and swam off, and he spotted her white, human legs.

He leaped off the noost, circled around it, and glanced up at the battle. Iron spearpoints crashed against leather-covered shields. Another sailor lay at Ulf's feet, holding his own guts, which looked like a ruined sponge. A second sailor staggered away from the battle-line and slumped against an upright standing-stone of the farm. The vanguard of the Sea-Bitch held their line as the spears hurled against them, and above them, and from behind their front rank.

To the crows with this battle. If Ulf gets himself killed, then I have no business here. Maybe she can lead me somewhere safer.

"I suppose I can," he said as he tiptoed over the gray berm. He skirted along the fjord alongside the girl, who swam in long strokes, hugging the coastline until she pulled herself up out of the water in front of the boat in the noost. She flipped over and crossed her naked legs, stroked the wet, flat hair out of her face and, with an elbow over her breasts, beckoned Asgeir over.

When Asgeir had come within arm's reach of her, he stopped.

"You're not a mermaid," he said.

"Maybe my fish tail fell off."

"Swimming around here during a raid," he said. "Are you stupid?"

"Why, would someone want to hurt me?" she said with an eye roll. "No, you wouldn't hurt me," she said as Asgeir watched her breasts jiggle beneath her dress like two jellyfish.

Asgeir turned back to the noost and, after one backstep, someone lunged up from the boat docked inside it. His belly clenched as he turned to run. *No! A waylay!*

Another had grabbed him from behind. It was two younger boys, and one shoved him to the ground. His head banged against a rock and sent a jolt of pain down his neck.

Before he could react, the boys were upon him with a thin heather cord, and he squirmed as they bound his ankles and feet, and all the while, the so-called mermaid laughed. She slipped back into the sea and swam away as the boys dragged Asgeir toward the boat in the noost.

"A pox on you vikings," a boy with a high voice said. "Harald will put an end to this!"

"That's right, Staale!" the older boy said.

"Harald?" Asgeir said aloud. His head throbbed, making him dizzy as he found himself slumped down into a small boat, just long enough for two oars. Blood dripped into his eyes.

Just what were they speaking about? Harald, the jarl from Rogaland down south, who declared no pair of snips would ever touch a strand of his hair as long as the kings of the Norvegr, the sea-route that spanned the length of north to south Norway, remained riven in petty kingdoms and jarldoms.

Asgeir gathered his bearings in the boat. They headed east from Rikheim, upriver. Staale appeared older. He had a boyish gaze in his green eyes and blond hair with a budding red mustache. The younger boy had curly chestnut hair over a hawk-like face.

"What's Harald got to do with it?" Asgeir asked. The boat slowed as a girl's voice yelled.

"Wait!"

The boat bent to one side as the girl pulled herself out of the water and aboard the boat, still in just a long hemp dress. It clung to her lithe body, her kelpy hair all aflutter in the breeze.

Asgeir saw no weapons among them. *They think I'm part of Ulf's crew. It's not my choice, by Thor.* "Where are you taking me?"

"You're our hostage! We got one, Beiner, we really got one!" Staale said.

"I wasn't a raider," Asgeir said, chilled from both his drenched clothes and his growing distance from Ulf's ship. "I was forced to be a deckhand, please, you have to listen!"

"Shut up, captive, or…" Beiner said.

"Cut your tongue out!" Staale said.

The boys rowed on as the bindings dug into Asgeir's wrists. He turned back to look at the beached Sea-Bitch at the riverside of Rikheim. The thatch of Ketill's house caught fire and lit up. Up ahead, the troll family stood stark against the green beard of the mountains. The boat went trollward as the girl held her arms and shivered.

"Harald will put an end to you vikings," Staale said. "He's tired of you raiding your neighbors and making a mess of everything, and so are we!"

"Yeah. There won't be any more raids along the Norvegr," Beiner said.

"I'm not raiding," Asgeir said. "I'm going to search for my father overseas."

"You bastard viking, no one wants you there!" the girl said in Gaelic. Asgeir raised an eyebrow at her, fully understanding the sentence. Her white lips curled in surprise.

"Stop speaking like that," Staale said.

Asgeir sat up, and the boat rocked. A salmon flipped several paces behind them. *I need to escape, but my hands are bound, so I can't swim.*

The girl slumped up against Staale, who wrung his face and nudged her away.

"I'm cold," she said in Norse.

"I don't care, thrall," he said, and nudged again.

"I'm no thrall," she said. "And your uncle Ketill doesn't like it when you treat me poorly!"

"If you're cold," Asgeir said in Gaelic, "then warm yourself against me."

If I can anger them, distract them, make them jealous, then maybe I can push them overboard.

As the boat floated around the bend, Asgeir caught the first scent of smoke from Rikheim behind them.

The girl refused to budge. "You said you're a troll."

Asgeir laughed that she said troll in Norse and not in her own tongue. "Trolls are warm."

"I said stop speaking like that, you stupid thralls!" Staale turned to them as he shouted, hacked up something in his throat, and spat first on Asgeir and then the girl.

Asgeir's face reddened as he wiped the spit off his face. Despite his grogginess, he wished to seize an oar and batter Staale's head. *But wait, me, a thrall? The son of the huskarl of the King of the Lothlend? A captive to the market of Bjorgkum?*

With all the anger of Red Thor, he pried at his wrist bindings, but the young boy had tied his hands up with a sailor's skill.

"They called you a thrall," Asgeir said to the Gaelic girl.

"Fuck them," the girl said in Gaelic. She shivered as she hugged her body.

"You're not a thrall?" he said to her.

"Nay," she said, "I was not born a thrall."

"They're going to sell you to the slave market."

"They said they wouldn't."

"They say that, but…"

"Stop talking like that!" Staale said.

"No!" the girl said in Norse. "It's my mamma's way, and you can't stop me!"

"I can't?" Staale said. He stood up in the boat and brandished the oar. The girl bent over and shielded her head.

Just as Staale took one unsteady step toward her, Asgeir leaned back and kicked him with both feet. The lad's shins smacked the rail of the boat, and he splashed into the water.

Beiner swung an oar at Asgeir, who cringed. The oar struck him in his shoulder, his arm, his neck, the softwood smarting his body. The boy raised the oar to strike again, but then a voice called out from the river.

"Help!" Staale shouted, his voice already a bit downriver.

Beiner stuck the oar out toward the other boy, but as he did, Asgeir kicked him in the rear with both feet. The boy flipped headfirst out of the boat, sank, and then bounced up.

"Help!" the two lads cried, Staale already drifting downriver while Beiner splashed and attempted to swim, oar still in his hand.

"That'll teach you. Why don't you drown?" the girl shouted in Gaelic, her face red, her gums bared.

Asgeir pressed the rail with his shoulder to raise himself, and sat on his knees in the boat. The rip of the current spun them sunwise. "We need to row," he said, "untie me!"

The girl fell to her knees beside him and wrestled with the knot, her cold fingers groping his hands and arms. "Nay, it's too tight."

"Is there a knife?"

The girl glanced about. Asgeir could see Beiner drag himself ashore on the east side of the river, while the little boat and Staale flew downriver back toward Rikheim.

"Nay," she said, "not a knife to be had."

"Helvete," he said in Norse, a bane-word for the Underworld.

"But look!" She brandished a fishing-hook and pricked at his bindings to loosen some of the knot. The boat's portside tipped, then the starboard side bent, and the boat felt like it floated over the surface. As Asgeir attempted to pry his hands free, he realized they were spindrifting.

"Helvete," he said. "Try and paddle."

She leaned over and, with a cupped hand and one hand on the rail, scooped up at the water.

"It's too strong."

"Helvete."

"We're going to die!" she said with a laugh.

Why would that be funny?

They plummeted toward a wide, bulbous rock. The girl screamed.

"Jump!" Asgeir shouted, as he dropped feet-first into the water.

His hair stuck to his eyes as he breached the surface of the river. Something pulled hard and long at his leg. An eddy?

Throwing his cupped hands shoreward, he thrashed his legs behind him as he launched forward like a ship being pushed. He found himself dragged back, his nose dipping below the murky surface, silty water oozing out from his mouth and nose. He tried again, and again, but something tugged him back, downriver, down below the surface.

"Thor, champion of men," he gurgled, "help me. My father is descended from your father, Odin. We are," his mouth dipped below the water. "Kin," he said as he raised his blurred eyes from the surface, the weight of the river weighing him, flowing into his open mouth.

Just as his head bobbed below water, he saw a leafy tree. His thews tightened, and he pushed himself above the surface a final time to find a bough drifting downstream. He grabbed hold of it with his still-bound hands, but his fingers slipped off its sleek surface, and he lost it. The river pulled him down, and he kicked his legs but without effect, like a tantruming toddler held aloft by an adult. He furled his toes and kicked smoothly, gracefully, and paddled duck-like. The river took toward the bough. This time he draped over it, its slimy, slick bark scraping against his armpit. He held fast onto it, sucked long breaths as he paddled shoreward, and— at last— found solid footing.

For a while, Asgeir stood there in the muddy riverbank among the reeds. His chest throbbed. With a snort, muddy water shot out of his nose and dribbled down his chin. He tightened his muscles and groaned as he pried his bound wrists apart until the rope unfastened and freed his hands.

I'm no thrall, those little shits! Just two days in Ulf's crew, and already I was captured. Helvete!

Upon a hillock, a house stood in front of a recently plowed wheat field. Behind it, the stark, steep mountainside. It all seemed abandoned, despite the smoke from the hearth. *The girl! Where was that Gaelic girl?*

A splash. He glimpsed a white shadow downstream. A mop of red over a body of white swam against the current. The wet head dunked under the water, vanished, and then came back up. The Gaelic girl, caught in the eddy.

He rushed back to where he had landed and grabbed hold of the bough. It was long, thick, and had three splits. It weighed too much to lift, so he dragged it until he thought he had reached the spot where he had seen the girl.

No red hair. No white body.

She must have drowned. How sad. A little bitch she was, but hardly anyone deserves to delve into the realm of Ran, where the drowned dwell.

Then something white bobbed up.

He shoved the bough out on the water toward her. She grabbed it and floated with it. He waded into the river after her. She flipped her hair in a shock of water over her head, her face calm.

"Lady Bride be praised," she said as she clung to her savior. Asgeir leaned over and pulled the bough toward himself, but it slipped from his hands. The Gael girl's eyes flashed in innocent terror, like the eyes of a sheep bleeding on the slaughter-block. Asgeir waded further until the current nudged him, and he leaned over and gripped around the bough just as it had begun to float away. He trudged backward as the Gaelic girl seemed to slide off it. She wrapped all four limbs around his trunk.

Crawling up toward the land, he tripped and slammed to the ground with her still clinging to him. They lay on dry, grassy ground, but she refused to let go, her cold body pressed firm against his, her mess of wet hair like skeins against his face, the ebb of the river over his feet and ankles.

"We're safe," he said, and nudged her as she curled her head closer on his shoulder, teeth chattering.

He gazed over her naked back. Her fawn-colored dress had been hiked up and tangled around her upper arms and neck. The curves of her hip and rear reminded him of the fairest maidens spoken of by the vikings that had visited his house, often with one at their sides. Each finger-length of her body in goosebumps, each rolling hill of her body like the undulating moors.

She scurried away as if he had been poxed.

"Don't you gawk at me!"

Red-faced, she struggled to untangle her soggy dress. He edged closer, but she slapped his hand away.

"Back down, you heathen!" she said with a sneer as she turned away from him and dragged the dress down and back to her ankles.

"You would have drowned."

She sucked in a sob. "You're right. By Bride, thank you!"

With a downward gaze, she returned and cuddled him for an eyeblink, but then drew away again.

"And stop looking at me! You saw me naked!"

"The river would have taken you," he said.

"You're not my husband," she said, redder than a viking's sword, "and I'm not your lady and I can't be your lady because you don't even know my name! My name is Éabhín."

She wrung water out from the hem of her dress. Asgeir did the same with his tunic. The wind blew eastward and chilled him.

"We should find haven somewhere," he said as he noticed his clothes stuck to his cold skin, "else we'll become ill."

"Bride," she said as she wept on her knees. "Praise be to Bride!"

"What goddess is that?"

She sneered as tears still ran down her cheeks. "My patron! She's of fire and marriage. But she's no heathen god, but a saint!"

"What's a saint?"

"Uncouth heathens—what have I done to deserve this?" she said, eyes heavenward now as she wiped the hair and tears from her face. "When a person is very good in life, they become a saint, and we pray to them for help."

"So you believe people can become gods?"

"Not gods, saints!"

"What's the difference?"

"A lot!"

"Like what?"

"You wouldn't understand!"

"Maybe you don't understand," he said, and offered her a hand.

She stared at it for a bit. Then her frigid, waterlogged hand met his, and she stood up.

"I asked Thor for the bough."

"The heathen god?" she said with a sneer. "Who the outlanders worship in the grove at Dubh Linn? You think he helped you?"

"He sent me the bough, and first it saved me, then you. You ought to thank him."

"I thank Bride!"

"Thank whoever, but let's get warm. I hope someone is home." He gestured to the house.

The two of them started up toward the farmstead. Its bowed walls stretched smaller than the other two they had seen. The lands looked fertile, with furrowed rows of plowed wheat, and the outfield overgrown with much brush and scrub. Someone toiled in the weaver's hut downslope from the farmhouse, and the pair started toward it.

"And what is this, robbers?" a shrill voice crooned out from the house. From her voice, he knew she was one half of the pair in the death-plot. *That was the woman that got out of Ketill's ship!*

Before them, two lean, shirtless men with scowls stood in front of the house like posts. One held a whip. The other drew something from his waist—a knife. Asgeir stood still as a woman with emerged, her white coif smudged in black.

"Burglars?" she said with eyebrows raised. "You thought us to be up at the saetr, hm?" she said, speaking a mix of Norse and Svear.

"Forgive us," Asgeir said. "I was taken in a raid, and the boat crashed. We nearly drowned."

She looked them over much like a mother would her misbehaving children. But her face hardened.

"You tried to swim across the river—serves you right. Well, we're not all up at the saetr; some of us are down here and busy. Go on then and sit down. Unbeknown to you, you trespassed upon the farm of Frida Two-Plait!"

Neither sat.

"I'm Asgeir, son of Hallgeir Gael-Slayer, huskarl to the King of Lothlend, Jarl of Eigg of the South Islands. I was taken against my will, and –"

"Hallgeir the Gael-Slayer, you say?" Frida raised an eyebrow. "What a tale! And the girl?"

Éabhín responded in Gaelic. "You stupid witch! I won't tell you a thing!"

"Éabhín, you idiot," Asgeir said in Gaelic, and Frida's thralls moved in closer.

"Escaped Gaelic thralls, that sounds more believable. Well, one of you is apt at the local tongue, I'll give you that. Japing or something more fiendish, are you? Perhaps the market will serve you two well!"

Asgeir and Éabhín turned to flee. The girl shrieked for Bride as the big thrall threw her down, and before Asgeir could raise his arms in defense, a thrall slammed him against the wall of the hut, his chest pressed against the turf. The air squeezed from his lungs as the thrall slammed him against the wall again. After a few more slams that left him breathless, he felt Frida binding his hand up with rope.

Bound again? Ulf, your spitefulness got me into this. I just pray to Thor that you live, and live free, so I might end that someday.

Frida glowered at them, arms akimbo.

"Just in time for the market today. This'll teach runaway thralls."

"You hag!" Éabhín said. "And why did you take me here?" she asked Asgeir.

Asgeir meant to respond, but something filled his mouth. A rag, punched between his lips by a thrall.

The second thrall wrenched his hand back as he yelped; Éabhín had sunk her teeth into his fingers. He danced about, waving his hand, and Frida chuckled.

"Redhead, bites, quite the vixen," she said as she cracked the whip against the hard-dirt ground, just a thumb-length from Éabhín's head.

The stench of piss billowed out from Éabhín.

Frida pinched her own nose and shook her head. "Even beasts can hold their bladders! Disgusting little thrall girl."

"I'll piss on you next time," Éabhín said in Norse.

With a crack of the whip, Frida lashed Éabhín across her thighs. She stifled herself as she clenched handfuls of her dress, but after a pause, shrieked like a mourner. Blood trickled into the pool of piss underneath her as a thrall gagged her with a sock. Éabhín gnashed at her gag.

Frida motioned to her thralls to clean up the mess, and they dragged Asgeir and Éabhín away onto the sward. After Éabhín had been cleaned, the thralls forced the two of them into a boat down at the landing place. The woman came out dressed in her finest clothes, and the thralls rowed them all upriver.

CHAPTER IV

The Thrall Market

Apair of thrushes sang from the trees above the marketplace. Stalls stood here and there with men in lavish copper-colored tunics bearing scales, their weights piled on coarse tablecloths. Children ran through the alleys of the tents. A shaggy, girth-horned cow from Pictland mooed, flanked by two men in green tunics that argued louder than it bellowed. Two dark-eyed men with a trove of reindeer antlers and buckets of tar served a cluster of patrons. Some small huts where women spun and wove dotted the riverside. And in the center, a broad wooden dais had been built.

Asgeir and Éabhín disembarked from the boat next to a row of tens of other beached boats. Frida's thralls led them by leashes to the marketplace of Bjorkum.

Frida wore fine clothes with her brooches at each breast, a festoon of colorful pearls, and a fine pleated, tansy-dyed tunic with a bronze key that dangled to show all that she was a landed woman.

"Two lost thralls!" she shouted as soon they reached the market. She rang a bronze bell, undoubtedly traded by or taken from monkish hands. "Two Gaels!" she shouted, and rang the bell harder, and now some of the merchants from the stalls eyed her. "Two Gael thralls—just into adulthood—who owns them, and who shall claim them? Who shall answer for their thievery?"

Asgeir spat beneath his gag. *I'm not a slave, I never was a slave, and I shall never be one. I'm descended from Odin.*

Frida's thralls shoved them throughout the market. Throngs of men and women came forth to witness the slaves. After some chatter, an older woman seated on a stool raised a wrinkled, gnarled finger. She wore a thick white shawl that hung slightly askew over her face, and a cat stirred in her lap.

"The redhead is Ketill Redcloak's," she said.

She is a thrall then, or was, if Ulf won that raid…

Frida nodded. "Then he shall have her when he arrives. But he must answer for her mischief! And the other?" she asked the growing crowd.

Asgeir looked among them. Two children chased a chicken and kicked up mud across his already muddy, still wet tunic.

He tried to mutter through the gag, but Frida spoke loudly.

"And no one recognizes this boy? Where has he come from? Who has claim?"

Silence.

"I've no need for spare hands—go on, get up there," Frida said as she jerked her thrall's arm. The thrall pressed against Asgeir, who stiffened his legs and refused to budge.

The thrall thrust a rocky shoulder into Asgeir. The lad dug his heels into the soft, muddy ground, and stiffened again. The shoulder strained against him, and when the thrall pushed with all of his force, Asgeir stepped backward. The thrall crashed headlong into the mud.

"I'm no one's thrall, and I won't be sold!" Asgeir yelled through his gag in a garble, but Frida's other thrall bent over, hugged him by the knees, and started to raise him off the ground.

The muddy thrall raised a balled fist, but Frida patted him on his hefty back. Instead, he helped the other thrall lift Asgeir and set him down upon the dais. A green-yellow weathervane fluttered over the treetops in the hazy distance. *The Sea-Bitch's weathervane? Ulf and his sailors back from the raid? If I just stall, they won't be able to sell me before he arrives…*

"A wildness about him— who will bid for him, then? He can make a fine warrior-servant! He is strong and young, but don't turn your back on a Gael!"

"You sell someone else's thrall?" a man with a local twang asked as he fidgeted with the headless hide of a marten.

"He skulked about on my property, Loki-like. Why, the two little trolls sneaked into my weaving house, and who knows for what? I am owed for this—and I shall take my payment from his owner in advance. Now, who needs a farmhand, a pick-hand, a rower?"

"He looks strong," the man with the marten skin said, and showed his palm dotted in silver coins. "I've use for him."

"What's that, five or six coins? A laugh! Who else? A higher bidder, perhaps?" Frida asked.

Some muttered among the crowd. A man in a salmon-colored tunic came forward and held up, with a proud grin, a smooth comb of antler. The sun touched bronze rivets of the comb as he rotated it between two fingers.

"Gift for your husband?" he asked.

"Masterful craftsmanship, but not enough."

Another man dragged a bucket forward, and his she-thrall with red-stained arms pulled up a herringbone-woven cloth of dark red. Madder-root trickled down with the murky water as she dragged it up halfway.

"Two ells of madder-dyed wool," he said. His she-thrall brimmed with pride as she struggled to haul all of the fabric from the dark-red water.

Asgeir's blood pumped hard in his forehead, and his eyes widened. *I will live through this shame, if it means I may avenge Odd.*

The sail of the Sea-Bitch came into view over the tents, the ship beached onshore, and many men hopped out of the boat. On the prow stood a figure in shining mail—Ulf the Old had arrived at the marketplace.

Frida cupped her mouth to speak, but people were breaking off and heading to the river. One by one, two by two, three by three. Even the owner of the madder- and pink-stained she-thrall walked away from the dais.

The crowd parted and just watched as Ulf's train marched straight for the dais. Frida backstepped off and nearly lost her footing. Asgeir edged away, but Frida's thrall shoved him, and the two thralls closed ranks in front of Asgeir. He peered through their hairy sides.

Ulf held two objects in his hands: a tattered red cloak and a tuft of brown hair. He led a train of men, first the bulk of his sailors, and behind them, a row of nine naked men with chains around their necks. The chained men had been bloodied, and one man limped on a foot that lacked toes. Erle, with a sweaty, blood-speckled face, hectored their captives up on the dais. The mass of bedraggled men smelled like eggs and shit.

Ulf the Old stood on the dais. He first held up the cloak that fluttered from his fist in three long shreds.

"What remains of Ketill's glorious host," he said, and dropped it. It tumbled off into the mud in a heap.

He brandished the ragged scalp in his hand. "And what remains of Ketill Redcloak!

"He and Gro plotted to murder me at his farm on Rikheim. They were to invite me there, where they would, as such gracious hosts, poison me with nightshade from Gro's garden," he said. "I thought I would go and thank them for setting up such a clever murder, so I decided to pay Rikheim an early visit to compliment them."

"You worthless vikings!" Frida shouted, her voice scratchy. "You have no legal right to raid in Haakon's jarldom—you will pay a severe penalty for what you've done to Ketill and Rikheim!"

"We merely defended ourselves," Erle said, "we are unashamed that Odin called us to war. We gave Ketill and his men the chance to fight, and we fought hard and lost men for these spoils, so we weren't unlawful."

Frida stood askance. Ulf eyed her.

"Don't give me that look," Ulf said, "you Svear she-wolf—we knew your mother sowed a foul seed when her legs parted for a bastard."

Whispers spilled out through the crowd. A woman wailed. Some men pointed at the dirty, downward-gazing prisoners.

"No talking to them," Erle addressed the onlookers from behind the captives, spear in his hand. "They're the defeated thralls, lucky enough to be spared. You can talk to them after you buy them."

"Where's Ketill's next of kin?" Ulf asked as he let the tuft of hair flutter to the ground, and the breeze blew it all over. "We already sold his whore wife and rotten children. But what about his nephews?"

"Missing," a man said.

The boys that captured me? The Gael girl did say he was their uncle.

After a pause, Ulf spoke again. "Why are you all so grim? You were already having a thrall market—here are some more thralls!"

Erle thumped his spearshaft on the dais as he stretched a hand to the crowd.

"Your friends, family, neighbors—they are in thralldom now," Erle said. "Thus is the fate of all who lose in battle. Now, bidders?"

Some men walked forward, along with an elderly woman carrying a bronze scale. Erle chatted with the crowd as the murmurs grew louder.

"Where is Jarl Haakon?" Frida asked, but Ulf stormed toward her. Her thralls started toward him, but Ulf caught sight of Asgeir.

"Asgeir? There you are! And I'll be taking him," Ulf said. "Just what did you do to him?" He unsheathed a small knife and cut Asgeir's bindings, then pulled the gag from his mouth.

"Ulf!" Asgeir shouted the moment the gag left his mouth. "She plotted too! She was the other woman!"

"Liar!" she shouted at him. She shot glances at the crowd. "My neighbors—do you really believe this lying thrall?"

Ulf nodded and grinned. "Lying, is he? I heard there were two plotting harlots, and we proved one already, and Gro met her end."

"What did you do to Gro?! All for what? The lies of a Gaelic thrall?"

"I'm no thrall!" Asgeir shouted. He seized her wrist, and she shrank back. Her two thralls stepped forward, but Ulf and a trio of his men met them.

"You," Asgeir said, wringing her wrist. She sucked in air and moaned, but kept her blue eyes locked on his.

"You and Gro talked about poisoning Ulf after inviting him to your home," Asgeir said, "and we caught you brewing the poison, and that's why you bound and gagged us!"

She wrenched her hand free and threw her arms skyward.

"Dare you accuse me of conspiring to murder? Dare you commit violence upon the sacred ground of peaceful Bjorkum? Dare you do so without the authority of the jarl?"

"Bloody Odin guided our spears to kill," Ulf said, and looked at the freemen.

The crowd had closed in around the dais, muttering. One man with a sooty face cocked his head and spoke.

"We don't need any more violence," he said to Ulf.

Ulf screwed his face up. "Frida Two-Plait will hang from the gibbet."

"Then by Tyr, god of justice, do it by law," the same man said.

"I thought you better than this, Ulf," Frida said. "You dare to kill the jarl's man and poor Gro and raid his home, and then come to the market to accuse innocent women of plotting murder? No one will doubt your evil then! Tell me, men of Laerdal, will you stand for this lawlessness?"

Grumbles spread through the crowd, and the same sooty-faced man stepped forward.

"No, we won't," he said as he adjusted his hat. "Ulf the Old, you ought to right this lawfully. The Thing commences in three days."

"Three days? I don't have time to wait three days," Ulf said, but the crowd hemmed in around the dais. Ulf screwed his face up.

"We'd best let them call the lawman, captain," Erle said, his eyes darting about the crowd. "Besides, we are the ones wronged."

"I suppose we've had enough war for today," Ulf said under his breath. He walked to the brink of the dais and addressed the crowd. "If Tyr, god of justice, will call upon the lawspeaker, then truth will reign."

"An assembly will set it all right," Frida said, "and your boy will be punished for lying. Luckily, the next Thing moot is in just three days—I take my leave, for I am in shock and, soon, bereavement for my friends."

Frida bowed and her two thralls flanked her as she walked down the avenue of parted freemen, her thin, pointy chin held high.

Asgeir untied Éabhín's bindings, and she tore the gag from her mouth until the band behind her head snapped.

"What laws do you barbarians have, anyway?" she asked Asgeir in Gaelic.

"The Thing moot, where all the freemen meet at certain times of the year, to settle differences by wapentake—that is, to vote with your weapon."

Éabhín huffed. "Even heathens have laws then—good! That hag ought to be flogged for what she did to me!"

After a short spell, Ulf ordered his men to fetch a chest from the ship.

"Spoils!" Erle shouted. "Spoils for sale, along with the newly tamed thralls!"

Half the crowd had left, gathering up their things, while other merchants went to their shops to prepare to barter.

Éabhín still stood near Asgeir, her face wet.

"My poor master," she said. "He treated me well. I'll miss him so much."

"They hated you," Asgeir said.

"Just his nephews," she said as she kneeled and plucked up a few tufts of Ketill's scattered hair that had loosened from the scalp. "But he treated me like a daughter."

Ulf placed a hand on Asgeir's shoulder.

"You've done well, boy. Speaking the truth is all we have in this world. Lots of liars about, especially these days. A weasel age, I fear. Treachery. Lies. Cowardice. Not you."

"She beat Éabhín," Asgeir said, "and tried to sell me as a thrall."

"She-troll," Ulf replied. "I believe you, boy. There aren't many Svear women around these parts, and you heard her tongue." He turned to one of his open chests with a glimmer in his eyes. "I have something for you. A reward."

Éabhín scampered about the ground, much like a hare as she hopped to catch stray hairs of Ketill.

"Reward me by freeing her," Asgeir said low, so Éabhín wouldn't hear.

Ulf jutted his yellowed front teeth forward. "I would do you one better, boy, and give her to you," he said as he ruffled Asgeir's hair. "But her value is high. Too high to give to you. But I see your point."

He beckoned Asgeir over to a chest. Ulf groped about and pinched a small silver brooch, circular with a long pin, between his thumb and forefinger.

"This is yours now," he said as he fastened it haphazardly to the split in the neckline of Asgeir's tunic. The silver gleamed like white gold.

"Let me trade it for Éabhín."

Ulf laughed. "Just like I was at that age! And no." And he walked off as someone beckoned him back to the ship.

She deserves to be free, back in Ireland.

He then thought of how close he had been to slavery himself.

Éabhín had gathered up a handful of Ketill's hair. She looked up at him teary.

"I thought you said you weren't a slave," he said in Gaelic.

She lowered her gaze and just gathered up more hairs off from the brown-green sward.

"Why do you do that? He let his nephews use you as bait."

"I don't want to talk now."

"Helvete!" Ulf shouted from the landing place.

The crew of the Sea-Bitch scrambled all around his ship. The captain himself ran up the gangplank and from the sound of it, went about overturning buckets and rummaging through chests.

"Helvete!"

Asgeir walked back over to the ship, where the sailors all searched about the deck of the Sea-Bitch. Svartganger darted away as they hurled objects, overturned stools, and tossed oars aside.

"You ought to not go about affronting trolls," Njall said to Ulf as he unlatched a chest.

"You ought to shut up," Ulf said as he unfurled the spare sail.

Tears. Rips. Knife-work.

Ulf shouted so loud that it jolted Asgeir's ears.

"Helvete!"

"Someone stole the tar. We have nothing to make oakum, nothing to caulk the ship," Rolf said. He lifted up a stool, as if a bucket of tar could have been under it. "And from the looks of it, knifed up the spare sail. Luckily our main sail was furled up."

"Captain, you did joke about not paying that tax to the trolls," Njall said.

"Helvete with the trolls!"

Some of the sailors gasped. Njall looked trollward.

"Someone stole our tar—must have been during the fight - Asgeir!" Ulf said, and pulled him by the collar of his tunic. "Just what in the name of Hel were you doing? How did you even get captured?"

"I got waylaid…" he said.

"Let him alone, father," Rolf said. "Asgeir could have saved your life."

Ulf turned his face, spat, and let Asgeir go. "Helvete—we need new tar. Come on—someone has to have some at the market! Clean up this mess—Asgeir! And thrall girl, come on!" he shouted back at Éabhín. "I said come on!"

The captain, Njall, and some other sailors all started back toward the market.

Rolf's lean hand slapped Asgeir on the shoulder. "Don't worry, man," he said. "You're just the newest deckhand on board. Father will lighten up with you." He headed down the gangplank as Ulf shouted at the wordless Éabhín until she came to the ship.

Asgeir and Éabhín righted the chests, stuffed them with their things, rolled up the damaged sail, and sorted the various stuffs about the deck.

"Slave work again," the girl said as she stacked some pitons in a chest.

"I thought you weren't a slave?"

"I'm not! It doesn't matter if I am now, because I am not, and soon I won't be, and I will never be again! And you heathens will regret it, by Bride, you will." She sat down now with a needle, a spool of thread, and a small sack of scrap-wool, and stitched up a narrow rip in the sail.

After a spell, some men returned to the ship and hauled a chest off, and Erle came back toward the ship and urged Asgeir out.

"Just you—the she-thrall fixes the sail—but bring that backpack—stuff it full of food."

When Asgeir finished the task, he left the ship with the wicker backpack. He found the crew at the market. Ulf sat on a brown horse with a blond mane, thirteen hands high: Ketill's former horse.

"Victory today—but still ill luck, a trade-off," Ulf said as he dismounted and handed the reins to Erle, who led the horse away. "No one in the market has tar, and the Finnmen had already left, so we are going up into the mountains to find them and get some tar from them. We'll need to rest today, but catch them. We leave at dawn. You're carrying our food."

Asgeir headed back to the Sea-Bitch. Svartganger peeked his head out from underneath Asgeir's stool. He strode over to the cat and pet him under his muzzle, and the cat purred.

So happy that you fare well, my friend. Today was lucky, but I fear what tomorrow brings.

He pet the cat until the little beast snored on his lap, and Asgeir drifted into a dreamless sleep. When it rained, he woke and wrapped himself up in his thick, undyed blanket, Svartganger snuggled beneath his chest.

"Wake up," Erle said. Asger found the sailor's hard, meaty face hanging over him. Svartganger curled his back and stretch-walked away and faded into the haze of the dawned deck of the ship.

Asgeir stumbled up and washed the crust off his face from a bucket. His eye had swollen shut.

"Yesterday was heavy," Erle said as he washed his whitened black hair. "You resent us, don't you?"

"I resent being taken from my farm," Asgeir said. He poked at his slit for an eye.

"Taken from your farm, oar shoved into your hand one day, a spear in your hand the next," Erle said as he gargled water and spat into the bucket. "Happened to me many years ago."

"And you resented them?"

"I did," he said. The crow's feet about his eyes deepened as he squinted at Asgeir. "Until I became the one someone else resented. But go on—get your backpack. Don't keep the captain waiting."

Asgeir found Ulf with a wicker backpack strapped to him at the foot of the gangplank. Rolf, Njall, and a third, bear-like man— Sveinn Foul-Farter— waited with similar burdens. They started off away from the river and up the mountain while the morning lightened. As the greens of the land hazed into browns, the switchback trail led higher up, and from there, the stony faces of the trolls jeered at them.

At a bend where Ulf trudged on ahead, Njall said to Sveinn in an undertone, "I'm weary of him jinxing our luck. It's unwise. We've just had a hard fight—luckily we won—and the boys are still whispering about that völva's hex."

Asgeir opened his mouth to speak. Had he forgotten that völva was his aunt?

Njall noticed Asgeir had heard and put a hand on his shoulder. "I don't blame her for being sour about the ordeal. She'll miss you. I had an aunt just like that, probably would have done a lot worse to Ulf than declare his ship's doom."

Soon the company rode into the tall mountains where the haughty trolls send rockslides, the sultry huldra lures men into the waterfalls, and the mirthful elves may wile children into their thralldom.

CHAPTER V

The Bear Fathert

Asgeir followed Ulf and his crew up the trail over the ridge of the rocky mountain. Grassy slopes stretched to their south, an endless span of rocky plateau to their north, and green tunnels of leaves to their east and west. The company followed the footprints of the Finns, identifiable by the tracks their small herd of reindeer left in the frosty mud.

Birds chattered about the trees as the company trekked up the mountain. The path became sleek, still wet from last night's rainfall. Treacherous tree roots and rocks passed underfoot until they reached a clear sward. Beyond that, an old rockslide covered in scrub trees. Just poking above the treetops from the ridgeline, the aft of the troll family stood against the green canopy below them.

The company slowed in the clearing as the land flattened. Ulf spotted Njall and Sveinn huffing like panting dogs, and held out his gnarled hand to halt them. He gestured toward the grass as he unstrapped his wicker-built backpack. Asgeir caught up to them, and gagged at the stench of Sveinn, who chuckled.

"Why do you think they call me Foul-Farter?"

Njall sat on a splotch of moss, stretching with a crunch. "My sea-legs are not used to this," he said.

"Feeling your age?" Ulf asked as he ran in place, his face red and sweaty, "I've twice as many winters as you, and yet this mountain hike is a stroll for me."

Asgeir leaned over, huffing a bit, centered himself, unstrapped his wicker-woven backpack, and spread out the food he had brought. The backpack had been heavy, and he had hiked hunched over, his back soaked in sweat. He sat for a spell, munched on some flatbread, and with the final morsel between his fingers, he turned to the troll family and chucked it down the hill at them.

If Ulf refuses to pay the tax to the trolls, then they get my bread.

Njall caught him in the act, and before Asgeir could say a word, the grayed first-mate winked and tossed half of his own flatbread piece off into the green yonder.

"It's known that a troll shows itself to those about to die," Njall said. "I reckon it's best to befriend ones already turned to stone."

"More superstitions?" Ulf said, and lurched over them. "I have never sacrificed to a stone, and yet here I am, the first up the trail! Besides, if the Wanderer himself disliked them enough to turn them into stones, why should I give them anything?"

Ulf laughed as he snapped his bread in half and chewed loudly with his mouth open. "We've been blessed by luck, so far. We won a hard fight, and I evaded a plot on my life. A three-day wait is not so long to wait for the handless Tyr to strike his justice upon my enemies at the Thing. We've been lucky. But that völva of yours still vexes me, boy."

"Why does my aunt bother you so much, if you don't believe she can curse you?" Asgeir asked.

"It was a slight in front of my sailors as they readied my sea-horse," he said, still chewing. "Now many of them fear her bile. Even Njall the Gray here is afflicted. We were well prepared for the sea-journey over to Hjaltland; now they cower like quarried hares. Yet, I am not so foolish to avenge myself upon the sister of Hallgeir Gael-Slayer. Your father, after all, holds power overseas, if he still lives." Ulf spat out the remains of his bread. "I can hardly eat knowing that."

"Knowing what?" Njall asked.

"That there is no honor now. In my time, if you cursed a man... or plotted his death..."

"We'll be going to the Thing," Njall said.

"If the lawman speaks true! Jarl Haakon is known for changing his mind as quick as the winds. He posted that venom-tongued Ketill Redcloak at the rivermouth to collect taxes for him, so the ground has drunk blood due to the greedy jarl. Tyr will mete out justice, and if the lawman disagrees, then Odin shall bloody Laerdal again."

He fell silent. They all did—even the birds quieted their chirps—and Ulf spoke again.

"Forget that loathsome harridan Frida Two-Plait! On with it, all of you. We need that tar!"

Ulf walked further down the ridge. The rest followed nine paces behind, until Ulf said fuck as the leaves underfoot sank, and he plummeted into the ground while soil and pebbles spilled down with him. It was if he had vanished downward from Midgard.

The company stopped and looked about. Asgeir could not no longer see Ulf—had the trolls got him? A muffled cry sounded up from where he had fallen, into the ground, in a shaft-like pit.

Rolf plummeted through the dried leaves, as did Sveinn, both in the same pit, a pace from the first. Asgeir and Njall remained aboveground, but the ridgeline was now suspicious, full of holes and unseen hands that could claw one down into the ground. Asger knew them as traps for elk that hunters dug in the uplands.

"Surrender to me!" a voice called out from among the mossy rocks.

Asgeir knew not what to lay down, since he carried nothing. But Njall unsheathed a knife from his waist.

"A man should always have a spear on the road with him," Njall muttered, and sized up Asgeir. "Have you a weapon?"

"No."

"Then use your wits. Find a stick or a rock. And take off that backpack, you will be quicker."

Asgeir unstrapped his burden. He searched for a suitable club or stone while a voice called up from the first pit.

"Just what is this?" Ulf said.

A relief he lives—I thought the trolls had their vengeance before I got mine.

A bowman came out of the green-gray gloom of the rockslide, opposite where they had trekked. He had an arrow nocked with the bowstring taut to his ear. He aimed it first at Njall and then Asgeir. He wore a simple, walnut-colored tunic and hood, tight-fitting britches, and yellow winingas.

"Guess who I am?" he asked as he shouted down at Ulf, iron-tipped arrow down into the pit. "Guess who I am of the one you insulted, of the one you accused of evil?"

"Let me out of here, and get that arrow out of my face," Ulf called up, "and fight like a man, if you are capable."

The bowman pulled the string even tighter.

"I should shoot you here and now for your insult against Frida—the 'loathsome harridan'!"

"Cousin? Wife? No—not your wife, her husband is not in Norway. Your lover, then?"

"My mother!" he shouted. He had a budding beard, but Asgeir recognized the youth in his face, and he reckoned they were the same age.

"Now then," Ulf said, his tone higher-pitched, the pace in his voice slower, "if you have an accusation, you ought to bring it to the Thing."

"Why should I?" he asked, "how unlucky for you that you fell into my elk traps, while I waited in the blind, to hear such an insult against my mother! I am Arild Rudolfsson, and I will not stand for that!"

"You may empty your quiver by firing at us in the pits, but what of my two men up there? You cannot strike them both down before one closes range on you."

The young hunter eyed Asgeir and Njall. His eyes flared, and Asgeir leapt, for he thought an arrow would fly. He had been right, for an arrow hissed past his right side.

Asgeir found himself running nearly on all fours across the soggy ground of the ridge. Another arrow sped past him and juddered in a tree trunk a fingerbreadth from his face. He scrambled past the narrow birch trunk and crawled away. He had seen neither where Njall nor the hunter had gone.

A leaf crunched nearby, and he glanced and spotted a pair of yellow winingas. He snatched a rock from the ground, spun, and chucked it hard. The bowman groaned as the stone checked off his chest. Asgeir armed himself with a jagged rock and ran straightaway for Arild in the scrubby rockslide, and an arrow sped toward him.

Asgeir ducked and landed among some mossy boulders, and all his limbs scraped about the rocks. An arrow hissed above and was chased by a second. He stepped on the granite ground to head downslope, but the surface was slick, and he slipped and tumbled headlong.

He heard another hiss. *An arrow? No, an adder!*

The snake hissed again and struck at him. He leapt backward, and it recoiled with another hiss. An arrow grazed his hair and sank into the ground below.

With a dry shout, Asgeir rolled over, but the snake coiled to strike at him again. *Two foes now.*

Red, fleshy fangs flashed as the snake snapped. Asgeir bumped against the berg. The snake rose to strike again, but before it could, like the snake, Asgeir snapped forward. He grabbed the serpent just below its head, and its meaty, wiry body writhed and jolted as he flipped over and tossed it overhead at the hunter, who just had nocked another arrow.

Arild slipped off his stony perch. In a thud, he landed awkwardly and screamed as the snake bit about him. It slithered and snapped over the folds of his tunic while the hunter tried to scramble away.

Asgeir ran up toward the ridgeline. The bowman scuttled back from the snake as it hissed away from him through the loose rocks. His father always disdained bowmen, for they fight from a coward's range, unlike the honorable duelist. Asgeir understood this resentment now.

"Listen, you bowman," Asgeir said, "if you want to settle this like men, then put down your coward's weapon! Face me in a duel!"

"Coward's weapon? Duel you? You little fucking..." the bowman said as he nocked another arrow.

To Helvete with this! I'll chance it in the mountains!

Asgeir had gotten up on the other side of the ridgeline, on the rocky plateau, and he raced off through he heather.

The plateau was colder, windier, and dryer than the valley. His heart raced each step while he searched for somewhere to hide. Hardly any trees grew, just heather, bogs, and bracken. Asgeir had run far across the plateau as the sky darkened and the mist thickened. He feared the mist, for many woodsmen, huntsmen, and fishermen had entered mist to never return. But it concealed him from Arild, and that eased his nerves.

In the summer months, women and children would head up into the mountains to graze the beasts on pastures before they return for the winter. Perhaps Asgeir could find refuge there, with a roaring hearth and a meal of milk and cheese.

I'll make my way over the sea myself—and find my father.

He followed a streamlet in hopes it would lead to a summer house, called the saetr. After several hundred paces, he came upon a maze of stone walls nearly as high as his shoulder. An old deer-run, where hunters had quarried deer to trap them since before the eldest burial mounds. He found nothing there besides bits of broken quartz. He slumped down against the wall, leaned his head back against it, and gulped in a breath.

After a few moments, he pressed on through the featureless moor.

It had been a long while since Asgeir had fled, at least half a day. He had left the food in the backpack on the sward, but the mist settled even lower to hide him from his enemy. He thought he had evaded his foe, but he knew hunters must be skilled also as trackers, and worried he would trace him and slay him like a stealthy wildcat.

He tiptoed around bogs, clambered over bergs, and scraped through the bracken and heather until he came to a sheep trail, marked by tufts of white wool that hung from stalks like ghosts in the wind. He walked the trail until twilight, when he spied some smoke billowing from behind a rocky outcrop, alee from the strong westerly wind.

A saetr? By the Wanderer, I can guest there.

Some gray beasts bent their necks into the heather around what looked like a white canvas tent. He first thought them goats, but when he neared, one brayed weirdly and he spotted their bough-and-branch antlers. Reindeer? The Finnmen! Wind-beaten, winded, hungry, thirsty, possibly hunted… surely, the Finnmen would not turn a guest away in his condition.

The smell of smoke and stew rose from the cooking fire just behind the conical tent. The reindeer stood in a musky herd nearby, side-eying him as he started for the camp.

"Hail, good Finns!" he shouted. "I am hungry, and there is a madman after me…"

A figure rounded the tent, and Asgeir gasped. He blinked once or twice, to ensure it had not been some turnskin elf that tricked him, and he had no iron to ward against it if it had. But the figure wielded iron in the form of a long hunting-knife. Asgeir noticed his legs were wrapped in yellow winingas. It was Arild, with a bandaged forearm and a venomous scowl.

"You!" Arild shouted, sheathing his knife and unshouldering his bow. He nocked an arrow from his quiver and pointed it at Asgeir. Behind him, a woman's black hair waved as she peeked from behind the canvas of the tent.

"You little shit…" he said. He unnocked the arrow and marched over through the muck-strewn ground, a handful of arrows in his hand.

"It can't be you!" Asgeir said, and withdrew a pace. "Fuck! I have no quarrel with you!"

"You won't run away from me. You won't throw a snake at me. You won't escape."

Asgeir found no quarter. The heather had been waist-high, the ground uneven, and the mountaintop lacked outcrops, bergs, trees or boulders to hide behind.

"Lay down your arms, we have no quarrel," Asgeir said.

The hunter again loaded an arrow on his bowstring and drew the arrow closer to his ear.

"That I would not witness against a man who would murder men trapped in pits?"

"So you may not avenge your lord."

The young woman behind the tent gasped. The hunter turned to her, and she stared back at him with dark, wide eyes.

"They insulted my mother," he said. "Helvete—they got away, but you won't now."

Asgeir now knew the others had escaped.

"I cannot stand to watch a murder," the woman said with a lilt to her speech, "and when my parents return, they will know of this, and not wed me to a murderer. Please, Arild, don't do it!"

The hunter clenched his teeth, relaxed the bow, balled a fist, and chucked the handful of arrows to the ground. They clattered about the hoofs of the reindeer that continued to graze.

"I suppose I need not kill you," Arild said. He started back toward the tent, but shot a glance back at Asgeir. He unsheathed his hunting-knife with its long, single-curved edge, and pointed it toward him.

Asgeir went breathless.

"See this? This was my grandfather's knife. It has been gutting deer since before you were born, and I will gut you if you don't listen to what I say. I distrust you, since your captain is venom-tongued muck. You're right, I have no quarrel with you, but I will if you dishonor The Wanderer by being a bad guest. Otherwise, I suppose you will be here for the night."

I don't want to be without shelter up here at night, either.

"Guarantee you won't waylay me while I sleep," Asgeir said.

"You have my word, on the Wanderer Odin, I would never transgress against a guest."

"But where are my companions?"

"The shits got away—but they will pay at the Thing. Insults must be paid in blood," Arild said. He walked toward the camp, where the woman waited aghast with ladle in hand.

Blast this Arild—he made me feel relieved that Ulf is alive. He's my kill…

Without anywhere else to go, Asgeir walked over to their camp, heart still racing, vein throbbing in his neck.

Food and shelter is better than braving the wilds. But don't think I won't give my word against yours at the Thing.

Arild sat on a stool in front of the fire and warmed his meaty, calloused hands. The woman stirred the reindeer soup. Twilight neared, and the air chilled so they could see their breath. Asgeir stood at the outskirts of the camp where the reindeer herded in the heather, along with a well-groomed, black-maned horse. An elkhound with mottled black-gray fur sat in front of the fire, ears perked and sniffing.

The woman wore a brown, thready hood cinched with two braided cords, and a heavy beige blanket for a cloak. She shot glances at Asgeir and Arild.

"You may as well sit," Arild said, and nudged a stool toward Asgeir. He sat, and they eyed one another for a while. The hunter worked to glue goose feathers to the shaft of an arrow.

"I'm Arild, son of Rudolf High-Hat and Frida Two-Plait," he said, lining the arrow to his eyesight to ensure the fletch was straight. "This is my bride-to-be, Sakka, of the Finns." The Finnwoman smiled.

"Welcome to our camp," Arild said and nodded.

"I'm Asgeir, son of Hallgeir Gael-Slayer, huskarl of the King of Lothlend," Arild halted his fletching and looked up.

"The son of the Gael-Slayer? Here, in my camp? By The Wanderer! I suppose I can trust you, but don't think I'll let my guard down. Hallgeir the Gael-Slayer—what a famed man!"

"Yes, I am his son. He always taught me to fight with honor—never attack an unarmed man, never kill a man when he is down, always give a man a fighting chance. I sought a duel but you just tried to shoot me."

"You tried to kill me, with that adder…"

"You shot arrows at me!" Spittle shot from his mouth as he spoke.

"Has anyone ever insulted your mother?" he asked with one eyebrow raised.

"They'd best not, or my father would –"

Asgeir halted his own sentence but then slapped a knee. "I never insulted your mother."

He had not insulted Frida outright, though he wished he'd done worse to her.

"Your lord did," Arild said, straightening the arrow again. "And he'll pay, especially after she finds out about it."

The wise man stays quiet, lest he make a fool of himself, Asgeir quoted the sayings of Odin. *In this case, I should stay quiet to keep my hide. Arild's too wrathful, and I doubt the truthfulness of his words. He shouldn't know what happened at Rikheim or worse, the market.*

"He's not my lord," Asgeir said. "I have no qualms about him dying."

Both Arild and Sakka glared at him.

"He killed my brother in a duel and took me from my home, without my family's permission," Asgeir said as his jaw trembled. "He needed rowers for his ship, and he claimed that our father owed him the labor. He came to take us from our farm. Odd refused and challenged his claim of debt by blood. We lost the duel."

"Then you hate him too," Arild said.

"I do hate him, but I want him to die by my hand. By honor."

"Why? You nearly were killed by my arrows because of that bastard!"

Sakka stopped stirring the stew, took a breath, and continued tending to the meal.

"As I said, I will kill him someday. Not arrows. Not the noose. Not poison, but man to man, in a duel," Asgeir said and nearly bit his lip.

"Regardless, he must pay for his crime against my mother. You'll be ransomed to him."

"Arild," Sakka said as she stirred again, scooped some out, and tasted the juicy meat, "why?"

"He got away because of this one," he said, and pointed to Asgeir. "They all did. And I nearly was bitten by the adder. If I died, who would be wed to you?"

Sakka said nothing as she sipped from the spoon again.

50

After a spell, she spoke. "Dinner is almost ready."

"It's late in the day," Arild said, and stood up. "I have not caught anything since hunting-time began, thanks to that old man and his band of shits. Ullr of the wilderness calls me to hunt."

"Sakka of dinner calls you," she said with a honeyed voice.

"Oh, shut up with that," he said. "I told you, I'm not hungry. I won't eat until I return with a marten or a fox."

"I spent hours cooking this stew—and when my parents return, they will ask where you are, and what do I tell them?"

"I came up here to hunt, not argue with you. Now shut up, you little bitch," he stood up and walked off in a huff. He mounted his horse that grazed among the reindeer and trotted away, whistling for the elkhound that then loped after him. They disappeared into the gloomed moorland.

Sakka wrung her mouth, and she continued stirring. "I can't believe he called me that! And left me alone with a strange man! If only my pappa were here! He'd get a thrashing!"

Bastard—he treats his woman poorly, does he? He misdirects his anger at her, just like he did at me, when it was Ulf who insulted him. His mind is like a whirling wheel—perhaps I should seek shelter elsewhere, or chance my luck in the wild.

Asgeir scouted about him and spotted the sheeptrail that skirted a narrow, icy ravine. That trail must lead back down to the mountains, since the sheep must return to their shepherd's farm. If his foe had gone off hunting, perhaps Asgeir could run away.

No, I'll stay. It's best to have shelter, my eye is shutting up from Ulf's whip, and my head still hurts from that waylay by Ketill's nephews. It may downpour tonight... and who knows what trolls lurk up here. I'll have this settled by single combat with swords, not by the coward's bow and arrow.

"If you run away, Arild will be even crosser with me for being a bad host," she said as she blew on the oily water in the spoon. He nearly balked at her words, for she was a Finn, and much gossip whispered about their magic, such as their drums that could beat the rhythm of Hel into Midgard. Did she hear my thoughts?

"It's unsafe in the mountains at night," Asgeir said, and truth be told, he feared giants, trolls, and Arild's iron arrows as much as the magic of the Finns.

"I'm worried. My family should have arrived now," Sakka said. "They were at the market in Bjorkum, and they said they'd be back before nightfall."

"A lot happened at the market," he said, but then corrected himself. "My captain wanted to find your people so he may trade. We arrived tardy at the marketplace, and they were gone already. We need tar."

"I've not known many of your people," Sakka said as she took a gulp of stew. "My father's father was fostered with your people, and he taught me Norse."

Sakka ladled some soup and handed it to him in an alder-bark bowl along with a small bone spoon. He shoveled the stew into his mouth and it dribbled all over his hairy chin, and she laughed.

The hot stew warmed him, and he savored it.

"Does it taste good?" she asked.

"Very," he said. "Maybe it needs some salting, but hunger is better than salt."

She laughed. They ate in the cold wind that howled over the moor. The firelight splashed the camp and lit the otherwise cloudy night; it spilled over her face, her sharp nose, her round chin, and her long locks of black, silky hair that curtained her colorless hood that covered her upper body. He wondered what she looked like under there, and if her hands were pale and delicate under her felt mittens.

"What's it like where you are from?" he asked.

"There are no trees, and we don't farm. The jarl comes from the south and demands we give him furs, walrus-hide ropes, tar, oil..."

"Walrus?" Asgeir asked. "You have walrus up there?"

"Yes," she said, and she leaned over and when she came back up, she had two sticks hanging out from her upper lip. "They look like this," she said, muffled.

They laughed. As they ate their reindeer stew together, she spoke. "In the north, in summertime, the sun dives toward the water and winks below it, like a curtsy. In some places, it's flat and barren, but in others, there are jagged mountains like scrap iron, where our dead are buried under cairns, before they come back as bears."

"Come back as bears?" Asgeir asked.

"Yes. We come from bears, which is why we walk upright like them. You know, my grandfather once saw an all-white bear? It was an ice-bear. After he prayed to it, he was blessed with big, fat salmon all that year."

Asgeir finished his bowl of soup and took a second helping, and then a third. He helped her take the iron pot off the fire, and the two of them piled some dried birch logs, bark-first, on it. Embers flew about as the flame flared, the wind blew colder and, shivering, Sakka and Asgeir pushed their stools together and huddled to warm themselves.

"You have no warmer clothes?" she asked.

"No, just my cloak, but no thicker garments."

"It's so cold," she said. "I wonder if Arild fares well."

Asgeir wondered about Njall, Rolf, Sveinn, and especially Ulf. Had they gone back to the fjord? Or were they freezing somewhere on the plateau like him? Would they set out to look for him? Surely, Ulf would have screamed for vengeance after they got the old sea-wolf out of the pit...

"I don't know where my captain or his mates are, or how they fare," he said, "just as I don't know where your husband-to-be is, or how he fares."

"Yes, my husband-to-be," she said as she groaned. "Our fathers decided on it last summer."

"Don't you love him?" he asked.

"He loves ivory—that is, the father of Arild does," she said. "Arild must love it, too. We're walrus hunters."

"You've come a long way from the north."

"I miss my home," she said. "But at least my parents are here with me."

"I miss my home also."

"Where is it?"

"Hordaland."

"Is it far?"

"Not at all. Just on the other side of the fjord."

"Then why don't you go back?"

Asgeir wondered that for a spell, and then shifted himself up. If he found that sheeptrail and started down the mountainside, he could get to the fjord by daybreak. Perhaps he could take some torches to light his way. He could, perhaps, even get back to Hordaland before Ulf found him. Why did he wait?

I must bear witness against Arild, even if I am just one of five. And Ulf did free me, after all. By Thor! I'd rather call upon my honor than admit I owe Ulf a thing.

"Must you go?"

"I owe your husband-to-be nothing," he said. "His anger is with Ulf."

"Will you really go, all alone, in the dark?"

The full moon seeped through the clouds to bathe the plateau in moonlight.

"There is a full moon," he said. "If the clouds let up, it won't be so dark."

Asgeir stood up, but Sakka grabbed him by the wrist. He yelped, since her fingers scraped a wound.

"What was that?"

"I got scratched up, when Arild was trying to kill me," he said.

She curled his sleeve up. The blood had clotted and scabbed, but she raised her thin eyebrows.

"Let me tend to this, heal you," she said.

Sakka led him by his hand into her tent, where the moonlight spilled in from the night sky, and the campfire cast dancing shadows around it. There had been a simple mattress and pillow, one man wide, a small chest, and some sacks. A long, unsheathed knife with a polished antler handle lay out on the lid of the chest. It was much warmer inside the tent, alee from the wind.

She took some mulched herbs from a small leather pouch and massaged his arm with the salve. He hiked his tunic up his chest, also scraped and scratched and full of pricks, and hiked up his trousers. He had bruises and blood marks all about him.

"You poor thing," she said. "Did Arild really do this to you?"

"My swollen eye and the gash on my head are not from Arild. But he was trying to shoot me like I was a grouse. By the good gods, either I'm lucky or his aim is shit, because all of the arrows missed me. I was nearly struck by a snake when I fell off some rocks and got bloodied up pretty good. But I threw a snake at him."

Sakka's mouth parted. "What?"

"I picked up the adder and threw it at him. That's how I escaped."

She laughed. She laughed heartily, like a drunken traveler.

"He's been chasing me with his snake—good to see the shoe on the other foot!"

Asgeir half-smirked. *I don't blame him, but he doesn't deserve a girl like her.*

"But that's how he got that snakebite!" she said as he winced when she rubbed the herbs along his shin. "Dent there, too."

"But he lied to me!" Sakka said. She stomped a foot on the carpet that spanned the floor of the tent. "I can't believe he lied about that! He said he stepped on it by happenstance. And I am to marry a dishonest man? What would my grandfather say?"

Sakka leaned her head against his breast.

I've never held a strange woman like this before, not this close. What's she up to? She's so supple, so soft, I like having her close.

"It's so awful what he did to you, but I like that you outwitted him. I'll mend you and patch your tunic. It's the least I can do."

He winced again as she rubbed more of the herbs over his arms.

"Your wit is sharper than his arrows," she said.

"He tried to kill me with those arrows," Asgeir said with a croak in his throat. Sakka gazed up at him, wet-eyed. "That adder saved me."

"No man should rely on a serpent to save them," Sakka said, and embraced him again, tighter. "I don't want to marry him, no matter what my parents say. I don't want to marry a liar, a murderer—a greedy man! Tell me, Asgeir, are your people all like him?"

If Arild caught us like this, he'd be stricken with madness. But I can't help but think he deserves that. He tried to kill me, and treats her awfully.

"Some people just don't have honor anymore. But our gods are honorable. Tyr set his hand in the wolf's mouth knowing he would chomp down on it. Tyr's hand was forever severed, but his honor was intact."

"What a god to have," she said, "I will pray to Tyr that Arild comes to his own honor."

She's impressed! She'd much rather have an honorable man than that dishonorable Arild...

"You should, a murderer is dishonorable," Asgeir said. "And I'll ensure the people of Laerdal understand that when I speak of his misdeeds in front of Tyr."

Sakka ran a hand down his twitching shoulder. "You said you hated your captain."

"I'll kill him some day, eye to eye, chest to chest, sword to sword. Like a man."

She pulled away from him. *A relief—if Arild barges in now, he wouldn't catch us like that. But I want her close to me again...*

Sakka knelt over and opened a wicker-built box, and she arose with a chunk of flint and a bow-shaped iron firestarter. She bent over a small shrine, just a candle bestride a bear-claw, placed upon a linen mat. With three strikes of iron on flint, sparks lit the wick.

"I light a candle to Grandfather Bear that you live long enough. May he defend you so you may fulfill your honor."

I've never thought bears to be my forefathers, and I hadn't ever seen a bear, save for their skins. But her eyes look so sincere...

"Grandfather Bear—my people believe in something different. Auntie Bjorg always said I had a spirit with me, present since my afterbirth. But why light that for me, and not your husband-to-be? Don't you care for Arild?"

She smirked as she cupped her hands over the candle flame. "What will your people do to him?"

"For his crimes? Outlawry. He'll be banished to the South Isles or Iceland or somewhere else, and Norway will be better off for it."

"But then I'll be outlawed with him!" she said, her eyes shined in wetness. "Must you witness against him?"

"My honor demands it."

And he deserves it.

"I don't want to be banished with him!" she said. "Grandfather Bear, show me a way out."

Sakka stroked the bear claw with her long-nailed finger. She stood up and approached him with downcast eyes and reddening cheeks. "Maybe Grandfather Bear sent you to me, because you have honor."

"Bears are never cold. You don't seem cold, but I am freezing," she said as she groped her icy touch about his hands, his legs, his arms, his chest. "No, you aren't. You're bear-blooded, as we say."

"Bear-blooded?"

"Bears don't get cold, and neither do you." she said. "You know Grandfather Bear watches over those that are bear-blooded? You have more of it in you than others."

"I'm a bit cold," he said as he dragged down his tunic, "so maybe I am not bear-blooded."

And I want you back over here…

"I'm freezing, away from that fire, cozy as it is in the tent," she said and drew closer as she picked up her cloak from the bed. She wrapped it around him, the wool of her undyed dress grazed against his hands. "Oh Asgeir! I don't want to be outlawed with Arild."

She's far too sweet to be treated poorly by that Arild, a whirling wheel of a man. She's treated me with nothing but kindness. Sakka! Maybe I'll take you with me instead. But I dread what would happen if we are caught in this embrace! I just can't help myself, she feels so supple.

As a lynx pounces, he seized her hips. They kissed, and soon he found himself on top of her on the bed. When her dress came undone, she was smaller and bonier than he imagined, but her legs went over his shoulders, her hair flew about her face, his muscles eased. He forgot his troubles when her ankles scratched against his ears, and the softness of her touch, and the rooting of his boar tusk in her underbrush, but he had thought it also vengeance against the hunter.

Never thought my first time would be in a Finn's tent while her husband-to-be stalked for prey in the mountains. This is unlawful! If we are caught, if Arild catches me… but I don't know if I could ever regret this.

The warmth of Sakka's lithe body, the silkiness of her hair, the way she squirmed, cooed, and sighed. He could not regret it, but shame did come upon him, for he lacked the right to commit that act.

"Arild may catch us," he said. "And kill me."

"Then I'd be dead also," she said, "and we'd be rid of him for good."

After a spell in her tight embrace, Asgeir failed to hear the footsteps outside until they had been upon the ingang of the tent. He perked up at the last footfall, but Sakka said "no!" and clenched her legs around his waist and squeezed tight.

Before he could wrestle himself free, someone ripped open the canvas door, and a man shouted something in a tongue he did not understand.

Asgeir looked up and found two people standing there, short, dark-haired, in undyed tunics. The man fell upon him, fists thrashing about his face, and Asgeir slumped to his ass. Each fist-pound smashed his face to and fro, his head reeled, and he found himself amidst rattles of knuckles, each cresting upon his jaw and nose and head like so many pecks of a raging rooster. In his fury, he lost his footing, and banged against the main post of the tent. Asgeir lunged toward the door.

In his daze, the firelight sobered him to run. He waddled away as Sakka shrieked something in their tongue as her father picked up a chest and hurled it at him. It missed and slammed to the ground and sent things sprawling. He picked up the knife that slipped from the chest, and brandished it at Sakka's father. All the while, the mother of Sakka wailed and, though Asgeir could not understand it, he knew she mourned for daughter's maidenhood. Sakka's father pursued him but slipped upon a sealskin that had spilled out from the chest, and slapped to the ground in a clap, and Asgeir found himself piercing the tight opening of the tent to the frigid moor of the mountain.

Outside, the reindeer had all been startled, and they watched him alertly. Asgeir hobbled away, trousers caught around his ankles, punch-drunk, the night sky spinning its constellations like the old priests of yore recorded them spinning by carving their patterns on boulders and bergs.

Sakka's father emerged from the tent and brandished a hunting knife. The iron blade shone in a moonbeam. Sakka chased after her father, her white, moonlit body clad in only a cloak, begging and pleading. She cradled her father's knife-arm, but he yanked his arm away. Asgeir, slapped even more sober by that, righted his trousers, tied them in haste, and ran toward the reindeer.

Clapping, shouting, he dove at them, skidded on his side, and landed in front of them. He sprang up hare-like, and the reindeer ran toward him, but curved away, pivoted, and then rushed toward the camp. A galloping din struck across the plateau as the reindeer all burst into a frenzy.

The Finnman pivoted out of the way of a running buck, its antlers wisping past his cloak, and Asgeir scrambled up the side of the outcrop and ran up it. The reindeer herded into the camp and, though they slowed and ceased, the Finn dodged and evaded their tawny bodies as they shambled about. Sakka screamed in her tongue, trying again to grab the knife from her father's hands, as Asgeir crawled up onto the berg, then found the sheeptrail.

Halfway down the trail, Asgeir retied his trousers as he found himself shuffling across the uneven ground. In all of his passion for Sakka, he hadn't taken off his clothes, and he thanked the gods that he had been still shod and cloaked.

Those shoes carried him far and fast as he glided down the trackway. He had humbled that bastard Arild, and now he had been freed of his yoke, and also Ulf's.

Nothing chains me now, neither Arild nor Frida nor Ulf. By Thor, the god of free men, nothing will stop me now! I have my revenge against Arild, and his mother, and Ulf will be next.

He flew over the bog, no mind to the night— where lurks the elves or the giants or the trolls— for he had sacrificed to the latter, and they brought him much luck.

I even stayed in the bed of beautiful Sakka.

When it dawned upon him what she had schemed, he stopped and coughed. *She didn't want to marry him—that was her only way out! To have another man's baby! I've broken the laws of Norway, to not sleep with another man's wife-to-be, and now they may force me to marry her! Fuck, what would my mother say?*

A vision of his mother with a face of shame came to him. He cried out, but found nothing but still darkness to answer him. He could do nothing but just carry on.

The moors undulated out before him: trackless, formless, endless. Shrubs and bushes scraped and rasped at his legs. The wind howled hard, but softened, and he knew that was an ill omen, for next would come rain, and that meant clouds, and that meant no light. Soon, the clouds shrouded the moon, and it grew darker. He iced his eye that swelled up denser into a slit with a clump of snow he found on the leeward side of a berm, but he found himself rubbing it on the gash on his forehead, his stinging nose, and his scabbing lips. His injuries dizzied him, but he caught himself grinning when he thought of Sakka. *Her father thrashed me good, but I will never forget her touch, both icy and warm.*

Asgeir trudged on, belly full of mirth, still clutching the Finnman's knife. His steps grew careful as he skirted a wide bog; his eyes darted about in search of a will-o'-the-wisp or other haunts that could spawn.

As he approached a ridgeline, a thorny bush snagged the wininga on his left leg, and it unwound. He stooped down in the cold breeze to wind it back up, but he glimpsed a shadow moving across the ridgeline. His breath squeezed out his tight lips, and he found himself frozen.

Nothing but a silhouette, yet it stood on two legs, bulky and pithy, with what looked like an elongated nose and a long tail. He just stood there, cold and steady as a drying cod, until the clouds thickened and the shadow vanished into the gloom.

Asgeir could neither scream nor yell. He wished for his mother. What would she say if she knew what her son had just witnessed? The poor lad had seen an omen of his death: a troll crossing the ridgeline.

An utter fear crept through him. The Finnmen would catch up to him, or if not, Arild would. The hunter was an oaf, but one skilled at tracking. Asgeir had taken something from him that he could never have again, yet who would have the last laugh if Asgeir were dead? He would never return to his mother again.

But I sacrificed to the troll. Why would it show itself to me like that? I don't want to die, not like this.

Nothing lay about him but the hazy distance, flat bergs, low shrubs, and the endless black-gray gulf of the four-cornered sky. He was lost, and it grew warmer— which meant rain— and it poured for a while as he trudged on. If he ventured back southwest to Laerdal, he would be apprehended. The Finnmen would not allow the slayer of their daughter's maidenhood to go unpunished, if Arild's arrows didn't meet him before that.

He prayed to Thor, the shield of the common man, to defend him against the evils of the wilds. *Thor, whose thunder fries the trolls, whose hammer smites the giants, whose leather-gloved hands reap up the very Jormungandr, the serpent that coils the world. The serpent is evil, and Thor will vanquish evil. Thor, protect me against this troll, because a troll means death, and I am unready to die, for I have to avenge my family, and return Gael-Kisser to us.*

Asgeir fingered the Finnman's knife. He didn't mean to steal it—he was a thief of maidenheads, perhaps, but not a thief of knives. Something dog-like bellowed from further afield down the moor. He groaned and turned to it.

The blobby shadow loped across the moor, splashed up through a bog, and leapt over a boulder. *A gray, shiny-eyed thing—what horror was this, no—not the unknown—a wolf? No, the elkhound of the hunter, Arild!*

The dog came upon him, shaggy and muddy from rainwater. It sniffed Asgeir and growled low.

"Shhhh," Asgeir said as he backed away. "Don't hurt me, doggy."

The dog's hackles rose up. Its ears perched, and its tail jutted out. It crept toward Asgeir with its black lips receded over its fangs.

"Don't make a sound…"

The dog barked.

"Helvete."

It had a throaty, rough bark, and it barked louder as Asgeir retreated further. He backed up through the boggy ground, the cold, still water pulsing up into him. The dog quarried him, taking careful steps, baying in rhythm. Beyond the dog, over the other end of the grassy ridge, two man-sized shadows emerged.

"Helvete."

Asgeir hopped out of the bog, clouded in midges. His feet fought against creepers and underbrush as he attempted to get some distance from the dog, but it splashed through the water after him, then shook water off its coat. It bayed as the two shadows turned into men. The clouds eased and revealed them as Arild, and Sakka's father, armed with a knife.

"You're dead, you little fucking bastard," Arild shouted. "You little fucking bastard!"

The Finnman too shouted something in his tongue, and Asgeir had no need to understand its meaning.

Asgeir walked backward, since he knew not to turn his back on the dog, or attempt to outrun it, because the dog would catch him, sink its fangs into a limb, and maul him until his enemies could come and slay him.

The land slanted as he trudged up a hillock, toward the ridgeline where the troll had stalked in and out of the shadows. At the bog, his enemies appeared under the moonlight in their heavy wool, and both brandished their weapons.

Arild nocked an arrow and aimed his bow at Asgeir.

"No," the Finnman said with a sneer. "Let the dog have at him first."

"Good idea," Arild said. "Raggi!" he yelled, and the dog's ears perked. "Raggi!" The dog spun and faced his owner, sat, and panted with his tongue lolled.

Arild pointed at Asgeir.

He can't kill me, because he knows there's a chance Sakka's with child. Sakka's parents would demand I marry her. But Arild? I could take Arild—

and his father—if only I had Gael-Kisser! But the dog—I must avoid him and that muzzle...

Arild stood just eighteen paces away. His face wrung into something akin to the dog's, with a wrinkled snout and cold, pitiless eyes.

Asgeir hit the rocky outcrop back-first. It felt hard and cold.

The hunter, now astride his dog, placed a trembling hand on his pet's haunch.

"Sic."

The dog wheeled to Asgeir, its lips vanished as its white fangs bared, it lurched forward, and raced up the hill after its quarry. Handholds and footfalls evaded him as he found himself groping about. A musty stench floated on the cool air. He tripped into a cove in the rocky hillock and stumbled into something soft. Furry. Not the wall at all. The dog sniffed around, growling at something beyond him.

The shadow stood upright, taller than a man, and bellowed a roar at him. *A troll?* His feet carried him away, for he had no memory of moving himself, as pure, stark terror struck him and he found himself away from that little cave. Something brown, pithy, and roaring emerged out of the cavemouth. It stood on its hindlegs as it waved its terrible claws at the dog. *No, a bear!*

"Grandfather Bear! You've come to help me!" he said as he sidestepped away from the bear cave.

Asgeir clambered up the side of the ridgeline as the bear snarled and darted at the dog. The dog dodged out of the way of its claws, and the elkhound, never a breed to back down from a fight, snapped and snarled at the bear. The bear lumbered at the dog and swiped with its hefty claw, but the nimble elkhound darted out of the way of its paws, and the dog barked back in such fury that the bear withdrew.

When he reached the ridgeline, the game continued, the two beasts pitted against the other, the bear and the dog snarled, snapped, and withdrew, while Arild whistled and yelled and pleaded for Raggi to heel.

My only weapon—I sacrifice to you, Grandfather Bear. Up on the ridgeline, Asgeir tossed the knife into the air, and it sank into the bog.

"Thank you, troll, for sending the bear—or maybe I should thank the bear, grandfather of Sakka, if she's right."

And if she becomes with child, that would be the great-grandfather. Asgeir found himself short of breath again. *That sly girl—she's going to get out of that marriage with Arild, and take me with her. But I do miss her embrace...*

He stole off into the night, deeper across the plateau, until the barks and roars dulled. Sure that Grandfather Bear had thwarted his enemies, he wrapped himself in his cloak, nestled in a dank rock-shelter with a dense underhang, and slept as it rained hard.

A throbbing in his head awakened Asgeir. He had found warm shelter in that small cave, bear-free, and his father once told him that if one bear had been around, no others—or wolves or wolverines—would dwell nearby, because only one beast would rove the plateau. He rested there, his face seared in pain as the rain pitter-pattered on the top of the cave, until a sunbeam lit his face. He imagined himself curled up next to the big, warm bear that had saved him, under Sakka's heavy cloak, with her lithe body pressed against his. He thought to rest more, so he turned and closed his eyes and drifted back to sleep, yearning for the Finngirl, the first girl he had known.

I'll escape this—and there will be punishment. But that Sakka! Will I really have to marry her now? The tricky, sly vixen she is. But when I think of the fieriness of her, I don't think it such a bad fate. But what will my poor mother say?

The notes of a woman's song fluttered about the plateau. They came in twos and sang sweetly, without restraint but still on-key. Asgeir stiffened—the huldra, the she-devil that lures men to their deaths in waterfalls, had she been at play? The troll had been just a bear, but what pranced about the mountains now?

Asgeir crawled out of the den and found the wet plateau no longer barren, but alive with song. Several girls sang from a stream nearby, and their voices carried downwind to him. They sang in Norse and not the strange tongue of the Finnmen.

Girls at the summer pasture! Up so late in the year with the beasts. *By Thor, I may find safety with them. Maybe they can help me get out of the mountains. Once I get to the Thing, that Arild will be sorry when all of Laerdal hears of his attempts at murder! Ulf would look upon me proudly for that.*

Am I really longing for Ulf? The bastard—he should be hung from a gibbet too, but at least he allowed my brother an honorable death. But the Thing—

will they force me to marry Sakka? Will they listen to me witness against Arild if they know I left an unmarried girl with child? And my head is even worse, first the rock when Ketill's nephews waylaid me, and now this. I may come to regret my stay in the Finn's tent, after all.

Red clouded his sight as he crawled out of the cave, and he staggered backward. Gathering his bearings as he blinked the redness away with his one good eye, he nearly spewed. He traced the girls' song, mindful about the slush in search of traces of human, dog or bear, but just found bird tracks. He could not see them, and if it had been Sakka and other Finngirls, then perhaps her husband-to-be and father stalked prey nearby, if Grandfather Bear had not slew them all.

The icy stream still flowed, and he crept down along its bank. Whatever lurked beyond the bend, he thought to clean himself, for filth encrusted both him and his clothes, and it was Laurdagr— the washing day— anyway. After he reckoned he had cleaned enough dried blood from his face, he set off around the bend.

Nine girls, ranging from eight to thirteen winters old, worked about a pile of tunics, blankets, and suchlike, and they sang a fluttery song as they scrubbed and dunked and then shook the fabric into the chilly breeze. Some bucketed water, while others stooped over near a pile of wool, some soap in a dish nearby. When one kneeled at the stream to scrub a garment, she delved into another song, and the others joined the melody. He edged closer, and as he did, one little girl with big blue eyes under a tansy-dyed woolen hat looked down at him from above the bank.

"Who are you?" she asked, then screamed, "It's the bandit!"

The girls shrieked. One lass behind her tossed an armful of garments into the air, and the wind sent them awhirl. Asgeir started through the streambed while the girls screamed and ran downhill toward the dale below.

"Helvete!"

The smell of smoke danced about in the air from afar. Nestled on a knoll among boulders, a small, square-shaped stone hut puffed smoke from its chimney. In the uplands from beyond the hut, cattle and sheep grazed in two separate herds.

Asgeir knew that house was a saetr. Why the girls ran down instead of seeking shelter there, he didn't know. *They knew a trail, at least. I'll run down back to Laerdal after them, and find the Sea-Bitch. Better to be among those vikings than Arild and his thralls!*

Hoofbeats thundered across the plateau, and Asgeir looked to see a horseman riding from the pastures in the uplands.

Asgeir ran for the slope of the mountain, where the girls looked like gray wisps in their white wool as they still fled down. He spotted the trail that snaked and then switch-backed at the ledge of the plateau downward, but he hadn't time to reach it. Neither trees nor ditches nor anything besides the streambed allowed him to hide on the flat pasture. The horseman gained on him: Arild, reins of his horse in one hand, and a lariat dangling in the other.

The coldness of the morning melted as Asgeir sweated, lungs heaving.

The huntsman rode hard at him, and Asgeir leapt into the streambed. He tried to slosh through the water, but found it too icy, and skirted about it. Arild rode to the side of the Viking-Gael and cast his lariat at him.

Asgeir dodged the lariat, though the hemp rope brushed his neck and landed behind him as he ran to the other side of the streambed. The rider again circled the lariat over his head.

"Come on, you little calf!" Arild shouted with a sneer. "You're not going to slip away from me! It's breakfast time, and I'm hungry for veal!"

Arild rode past him. Asgeir crossed the slippery, icy stream as the rider steered his horse back toward him, kicking up whitened clods of mud in its wake. The musk of the horse filled the chasm as the steed stepped across the ice, its hoofs breaking through the thin sheets, and it crashed through after Asgeir.

"Dismount," Asgeir said, "and fight like a man. Duel me, Arild!"

"You get no such honor, you wedding night's thief! I'll trample you dead!" Arild dug his heels into his horse and charged Asgeir at a gallop.

Asgeir scrambled up the streambed and ran down across the plateau, back toward the sheeptrail that led down the mountain. Arild's horse neighed as it nearly stumbled into the stream. It righted itself, and tiptoed on. The hunter swore something black and goaded his steed into a trot across the streambed.

Luck be with me, I can get away...

He would have to scrape down the steep slopes, avoiding the trail entirely. The horse couldn't follow him, though Arild could. Asgeir could maybe outrace him, but not his horse. Two shapes paced down the trail from the saetr. They looked like thralls, stripped to waist and mottled in sweat and mud, one armed with an axe, and the other a wooden-bladed shovel.

Outnumbered now, too. By Thor—is Sakka really worth this?

The clouds parted, and the wind blasted Asgeir as he ran northward. The rider gained on him, the hoofbeats loud claps, louder and louder as Asgeir took gulps of breath. His lungs clasped, his feet heavy as the weariness of the last few days pressed on him. He raced for the slope, a steep, scrubby drop below. It was his only chance. The horse would not follow him on such treacherous ground.

When he reached the very end of the mountaintop—to his right, the trail, to his left, the slope—he felt the lash of wind as the lariat sought him. It snapped against his back as Arild grunted. That smarted, but at least it hadn't fallen around his neck. The horse slowed at the ledge and Arild steered his steed toward the trail as Asgeir led him toward it. *Run for the trail, but then veer into the scrubby trees and flee downslope. Pray to Thor that I don't fall too hard…*

Arild goaded his horse on, but his steed refused, neighed, and rolled his eyes. Asgeir shimmied feet-first down the slope, finding grips on rock ledges and footfalls in frosty dirt. When he glanced over toward the trail, the two hulking thralls were approaching him.

The he-thralls reached the trail, and were upon him. Some tumbledown halted his path, and as he pivoted, the shovel swung at him in an arc and thunked against the hard earth right near his head.

His heart wrenched in his chest as dirt trickled into his eyes from the wool-wrapped feet of the thralls above him.

"Enough," Asgeir said. "Arild, duel me to end this!"

The other thrall grunted as he raised an axe overhead with a finely polished blade and slammed it at him. Asgeir rolled out of the way, and the axe crushed the earth beneath its swing.

"You're all mad murderers!" Asgeir cried through his teeth. "You sons of bitches!"

Asgeir skidded down the scrubby, slushy hillside. He sidestepped around rocks and heather as he found the muddy ground nearly slippery enough to ski.

The thralls muttered something fierce. They both trekked down gingerly, rocks shifting under their feet, and they found no secure footings. Asgeir laughed at them—he could just slide down away from them. He caught his breath as he started to round the pile of tumbledown.

Something draped over his head. Harsh, rough, piny. It tightened and the wind squeezed out of his throat. He clasped it—a hemp rope—and lost his footing. Something dragged him up the hillside by his neck until he dangled from a noose, kicked his legs, and retched a scream but nothing came out. His eyes darted and landed on a figure sure-footed in the slush: Arild ahorse and his two thralls with two-handed grips on the lariat.

"I can hang you here and now," he said, and Asgeir swung a bit. The rope dug into his neck and with all his might, he sucked on the wind, but nothing went through. His lungs convulsed, and his chest tightened. Pure stark fear shot through him and settled. *I am going to die...*

"I can just let you hang," Arild said, "but that is too good of a death for you."

Asgeir found himself higher, lifted, dragged up the frosty slope of the mountaintop and back onto the frost-hard pasture. The stream tinkled beside him as the noose loosened. He caught his breath in gulps, as if he drank the air, and grasped his raw, bleeding throat with his own hands. For an eyeblink, he thought he owed Arild thanks for allowing him to breathe again. Then he sucked in a last wind, and relaxed his hands.

Before he could react, a felt-covered foot kicked him in the chest, and he slipped and landed on his ass. Arild's face leaned in and blocked out the sun, his messy dark hair like vines that dangled from his fur-lined cap, his forehead lined in pulsed blue veins, his eyes like two blue burning coals.

"I could torture you to death, and so could Gealbu."

Asgeir reckoned that Gealbu was Sakka's father.

"I have no more words," Arild said.

Arild lobbed the lariat to his nearest thrall and swung onto his black-maned mount. Raggi ran to them, tail wagging, until he spotted Asgeir. The dog snarled, but Arild shushed him.

The thralls fell upon Asgeir, one locking his elbows behind his head while the other had his legs. They tied him up, hoisted him into the air, and slumped him belly-first over the backside of the horse.

Sweat dripped from his head as he lay there, the bristly coat of the horse scraping his face with each step. The northern wind hammered down and he shivered and sweated, the warmth of the horse his only hearth as the rider carried him to the downward trail, followed by the thralls and dog.

Thor hasn't saved me. Not yet. But perhaps he will allow his half-brother, Tyr, to deliver my revenge at the Thing.

They descended the mountain, path by path. Asgeir raised his chin off the horse to look down below before the trees grew too tall. There, he found the river, and the wide rut where the oxen and men had dragged the boulder out of the waterway.

Perhaps I was hasty with that Sakka. But to Helvete with this Arild—I'll have my revenge on him yet. Once I get back to Laerdal it'll be all right, for the gods love me, as Auntie Bjorg always said. I'm the son of the huskarl to the King of Lothlend, and Tyr will stand at my side.

The birch trees soon covered his vantage, and Arild spoke.

"I would love to hear your neck snap," he said through his teeth, but then let out a laugh. "But Mother wants you alive."

Frida's farm stood on a hillock down in the valley, billows of smoke puffing from its chimney. The wall of mountains lay beyond, and then, blue sky. Green mountain, blue sky, white smoke.

He thought of the bear that had saved him. The forefather of Sakka. But where was that bear now? Perhaps it wished to have vengeance on him for what he had done to the daughter of its people? What of Ulf and his men, would they come for him? And Svartganger! He missed the cat, such a good little mouser. He cherished these thoughts as he enjoyed the warmth of the horse against the bitter wind, until they came down from the mountain and reached Frida's farm.

CHAPTER VI

The God of Justice

T he Norns have spun something weird," Frida said as she eyed the bound Asgeir. He was being held captive inside the weaving hut. His legs had gone numb, and his fingers hardly tingled.

Caught again by Frida! Where is my fylgja to guide me away from her? Why have I become snared by her and her kin?

Candlelight danced by him as two she-thralls stacked another two dried turf blocks onto a pile.

"The Norns spin the fate of all men on Midgard. Your thread must be frayed and hooped. How can one young man cause so much havoc?" she asked as she sat in a chair, eying him as she wove a fat bone-needle through a half-finished sock.

"There is so much work to be done. So much wool to be threshed. So many udders that need milking. You scared my thralls all the way down the mountain, like spooked deer. We're so far behind, and it's nearly the last slaughter. And that is just the crime you committed since dawn. My son is a hunter, and he tracks, traps, and hunts well. We promised a fox or a marten would line the hood of Sakka, his bride. You ruined that," she said, nonplussed, as she bound more thread onto the green sock. "You ruined too much."

The twine chafed his wrists as he balled his fists. *I hate you! It's you whose thread I have been wound in, when you plotted to murder Ulf! You and your son are rotten fruit from the same diseased tree.*

Frida wound and bound the sock with the thick bone needle. The light danced about her blond locks under her linen wimple while she leaned back on the chair. The she-thralls toiled about at a table, chopping onions and carrots for the midday soup.

"You would have been a murderer, and so would your son. How could you?" Asgeir asked.

"How could I? You're a wedding night's thief," she said. "You're the puppy of a rampaging, crazed old dotard that has brought the fires of Muspelheim to our humble Laerdal."

"I didn't want any of this. I should be back on my farm preparing for the slaughter. Yet you're still a would-be-murderer."

"Last night's crimes will ring louder than your accusation."

"You have no honor."

She stopped her binding, and looked up at Asgeir. "I have no honor? I, who had left my home as a young soil-girl, not at the behest of my father, but of my own will? I, who volunteered to marry Rudolf High-Hat to ease the war between the Geats and the Svears? I, who stay loyal to my husband, though he can never set foot along the Norvegr again? I have no honor? And which adder hisses that at me? The dirty polecat that made the beast with two backs with an innocent, unwed maiden?"

She's right—by Thor—she's right. What was I thinking? Blast it! I have none to blame but myself. But that sweet Sakka—Arild doesn't deserve her!

With that last word her voice cracked, her twang thickened, and she slammed the needle and sock down on the hard-dirt floor.

"The charges against you are as long as the serpent of Midgard!"

"And you're the venom he spits," Asgeir said, surprising himself.

"I will not hear another word," she said. "Ketill was a friend. And my dearest friend, Gro, I am bereaved for them both." Her eyes looked glassy in the firelight. "You don't know what Ulf had done to my husband. He had no right."

Asgeir wriggled in his bindings as the Svear lady rose from her seat and snatched a kitchen-knife off the table. She plunged the blade into the turf foundation of the house.

"How I wish I could stab that Ulf! He had no right!"

If Arild would murder him, so would his mother. He tightened his legs to stop his bladder from emptying. *I don't want to die like this... Thor, defend me!*

She sat back down and eyed Asgeir, who breathed heavily through his nose. Perhaps it would have been better for her to stab him, if she had planned to torture him to death, as Arild had guaranteed. *Thor would divert the knife toward my heart, rather than my gut, I think.*

"You had no right," she said.

A stinging crept up around his neck from Arild's noose. And that was when he became aware of the swollen nose and roving headache that Gealbu had inflicted on him. His eye had slitted even thinner and he could hardly see out of it. All of his wounds surged over him.

"That is my son's wife-to-be! What if she is with child now? Are you grinning? Are you proud of what you did?"

"No," he said.

"I ought to make you regret it," she said as she glanced over at the knife. "But the Thing will decide your fate. The gods love the lawful. Her father will be joining us, though Finnmen are rarely permitted at our moots. I will ensure the Finnmen bear witness to your misdeeds. Yes, you will pay dearly. Tell me, who was your father again?"

"I told you, Hallgeir Gael-Slayer, huskarl of the King of Lothlend."

She huffed. "I was wrong to assume you were a Gael. Well, the last news I heard, your father was down in Ireland. Ireland is just a few stepping-stones from Orkney. My husband will hear of this, and your father will pay for your punishment. The Thing will ensure of that! And shame on you! The son of Hallgeir the Gael-Slayer, a humper before marriage!"

Asgeir squirmed in his bindings, for now he realized his mother would hear about his stay in the Finns' tent. All the gossip of the Norvegr would be about how the son of the Viking-Gael whelped a bastard on the Finnmen! His face flushed warm and he wished to escape, yet there was no chance to avert his fate.

"What's wrong?" Frida said, sneering. "I'd be so embarrassed. If you were my son, I'd never want to see you again!"

Asgeir squirmed harder. She stuck her head out the open door of the hall and whistled.

"Maybe I should visit your mother personally and tell her what you've done—nay, maybe Sakka should be shipped out there to tell your mother every single filthy little detail..."

He thought of his poor mother at the landing place when she watched Ulf take him away while Odd's lich was still warm. How many troubles did she need? Asgeir retched.

"Ponder what your mother will think! I'm off to send a messenger to my friend in Trondheim, and another in Avaldsnes, and yet one further to Lofoten, and all of Norway will hear the news about the son of Hallgeir the Gael-Slayer who deflowered that Finngirl!"

She stood up and left. The breeze blew into the small hut and chilled him as she shut the door. He sat for a long time in the dark and thought of Tyr.

Tyr, one-handed god of justice, defend me. Whatever wrongs I have done have been heaped upon me threefold by Arild.

He found himself missing Sakka. Her icy but still warm touch would soothe him now.

The day grew colder as he sat there in the hut into the later evening. He dozed in and out in his dizziness, with claw-like throbbing in his neck and head. The gleaming, gleeful dark eyes of Sakka haunted him. He groaned when he thought of her with child, but that silky hair, that white, lean body, those legs wrapped around his waist. *I somehow cannot find myself angry at her, as much as I would like.*

One of the he-thralls— a bucktoothed, balding redhead with a flat nose— opened the door and dropped a wooden bucket along with some linen-wrapped object. The thrall untied his bindings with rude hands and left. Asgeir found bread and butter inside the linen, and he ate slowly to ration it.

The last gleams of sunlight spilled in through the crevice between the door and the hut. Asgeir warmed his face in the sun for a while. Something stole about outside the small wooden door. It sniffed and stalked about. A lapdog? Asgeir then caught a glimpse of red, the fox Nosey, marked by the patch of white on his neck.

Good to see a familiar face, Nosey! My heart warms for this cute fox! Auntie Bjorg always said my guide that appeared from my afterbirth—my fylgja—would watch over me.

"Are you my fylgja, Nosey?"

He broke off a piece of the flat bread and tossed it out through the crevice in the door.

Nosey sniffed it, snatched it, hopped back away, and settling by a bush, gnawed at the bread. He swallowed and looked about, and Asgeir tossed another piece to him. The fox walked up to the door, and holding a piece of bread between his fingers, Asgeir fed him. The wet nose of the little beast brushed his hand, and its fangs scratched his finger. He pulled his finger back and waved his hand.

Hoofbeats pounded outside. The fox halted chewing and froze in place. Asgeir spied Arild's black-maned horse, with the hunter mounted upon it. He slapped the flank of his horse with a pizzle, and they turned around Frida's longhouse and started toward the hut.

I remember he said he was in the mountains hunting for a marten or a fox—oh, fuck! He'll find a fox pelt here!

Asgeir shoved his shoulder against the door and lurched it open a hair. It creaked as he piled his weight into it. The bottom of the door trudged through the hard-dirt floor of the entryway and strained on its hinge against the force of the chain that held it closed, until it opened in a slight gap.

"Come in, little friend," he said with a strained undertone. "You can hide here."

Nosey's glazy eyes just looked up at him. The fox started to turn away, but then the sound of hoofbeats echoed louder. Nosey's furry hide brushed against his legs as the kit trotted right into the hut. Asgeir released the door, and it slammed shut. The horseman rode over.

"What were you doing?" Arild asked him through the door. "You little shit! Are you trying to escape? That chain was made by my father, no chance for you to break it."

"I just needed some fresh air, calm yourself," Asgeir said.

"Don't you dare tell me to do anything. Listen, I just saw a fox—did you see it pass by?"

"No."

"Really? I thought I saw something run by here," he said, and dismounted. The horse walked off as he bent over and scanned the grass, still holding the pizzle.

"Something just ran in here, looks like a paw print. I'm going to beat you with this bull cock for lying."

Arild undid the chain and opened the door. The light from the sun silhouetted him while blinding Asgeir. The latter backed off as the former entered the house, leaving the door ajar behind him. His eyes searched in all directions.

"It may have been a cat," Asgeir said. "A fox wouldn't run in with me in here. It must be a cat—I just didn't see it. It probably ran off."

The huntsman said nothing for a while, stroking his brown, scraggly beard, and walked about the house.

"That was a fox's pawprint, but I suppose even an idiot like yourself can be right once in a while. The fox must have run past the hut when it heard you stirring about. But Pussycat is in there?" Arild said. "Here kitty kitty! Come out, Pussycat!"

Something shuffled behind a long, green, woven cloth hanging on a rack near the loom. Arild bent over and stuck his hand under it. "Here kitty kitty…"

"Ow!" Arild yelled. "Ow, ow, ow!" The cloth slid off, and there Nosey had Arild by the finger. The eyes of the fox slitted, and his ears bent as he snarled. Arild wrenched his hand around as the fox held steadfast, his snout engulfing the hand. Arild dropped the pizzle, and it rolled about as the fox released his hand and sped off past Asgeir, and scurried out the door.

Arild screamed as he held his pulped forefinger. The blood spurted out, staining darkly all over his coat and tunic and splotching the floor.

"You son of a bitch!" Asgeir shouted.

Asgeir rushed over as Arild staggered around the hut. He seized the knife in the sheath that hung from Arild's belt, drew it, and shoved his foe. Arild slammed to the ground and spun over, to find the sharp edge of his own knife prodding his throat.

"I should kill you," Asgeir said. "I should slash your throat here and now and then go and hump Sakka again, send her screaming into the night again, and I should slit the throat of your wren of a mother, too." Arild lay there wide-eyed.

"But I want honor," he continued. "My father always said to never kill a cowering man, to always seek to give the defeated a fair chance to fight. We will settle this like men. At the Thing, you're going to propose we agree to a duel, so all know our pact. We end this outlawry, and so duel we will."

Arild had been biting his own lip until it dribbled blood.

"Do you agree or not? Duel or not? Duel me, or I will slice your throat."

He pressed the cold, black-veined blade into the skin of Arild's neck.

"I swear," Arild said as he breathed in stunted pulses. "I swear an oath that I will fight you in a duel to end this."

"Swear it on the grave of your grandfather, your odalmann. Swear it by the mound that gives you your land."

"I swear on the green mound that grants my land to me," Arild said, "by the grave of my grandfather: at the Thing, I will accept your challenge to settle this by duel."

Asgeir stood up, and put his hand down to him. Blood had spotted the floor. Arild's wet palm met his, Asgeir helped him up to his feet, and wrung his lips as he saw Arild's grated finger.

"I'm sorry for your wife-to-be," he said. "I pray that she is not with child."

Arild stayed silent.

For a spell, Asgeir remembered the hooves of Arild's horse that had pounded about him as he fled from the lariat. He remembered how he had hung like a sacrifice to Odin. He remembered wheeling and dodging and ducking from hissing arrows from the yew bow. He remembered the waylay, when his comrades had vanished into pits in the ground. Arild, you son of a fucking bitch.

Asgeir bent over, picked up the pizzle, and whacked it across Arild's thighs. The huntsman yelped.

"Go get help, you idiot!" Asgeir said.

"Mamma!" Arild shouted. "Mamma, help!" He then ran to the door. Two he-thralls armed with wooden clubs rushed to the open door. Arild ran past them, holding his finger, and caused much commotion back at the farm as he ran toward it.

The he-thralls started toward Asgeir, but he slammed the door shut in their faces, and barred it with the pizzle. *I'll bide my time until the Thing.*

He slumped down into a corner. *Even someone like Arild will uphold an oath. The son of a bitch.*

There was little less sacred for his kind than an oath, and they all knew oathbreakers faced the worst hereafter, for the gods hated those that broke their oaths.

We've gone blow for blow now. He hunted me down twice, but I forced him to settle it by sword, not mischief, false speech, or guile. Fuck him, to Helvete with him! May Ullr guide me so I may send him to the afterlife.

A duel at the Thing. Surely, my father would be proud, since he is such a skilled duelist that the King of Lothlend made him a huskarl. Honor returns to me—I'm so tired of all this skulking about. Just what would Ulf have to say? Fuck! I don't want his advice. Or maybe I do… he is a formidable opponent.

Odd, you will not go unavenged. First, I will defeat Arild, then when the gods decide, Ulf.

After the sun set, he found himself crouched in the corner. He had dabbed up the blood and shreds of flesh with the green blanket. "Ullr," he said as he nestled in a corner. "I will sacrifice mightily to you if you are on my side, even if you were not on our side when we lost to Ulf and Rolf."

Ullr, the god of duels, bestow upon me your power, for I am an honorable man who could have slaughtered Arild in revenge and in protection of myself. But I chose the duel, to please you, the god of duels and honor.

Asgeir prayed similarly all night until he drifted to sleep.

In dreamtime, Asgeir wandered down the byway of a dense forest. He trekked over thorns and brambles underfoot. Dew dripped off leaves, and birds chirped around him. In the green gloom of the forest, a deer bent its neck down to graze. In a twang, an arrow soared through the air and feathered the deer's neck. Stalking in the forest and stepping on the byway, Asgeir found the bowman.

A handsome young man with a long, yew-staved bow stood before him, clad in a soft, green tunic and tight, brown trousers, a leather quiver strapped around his shoulder. He lowered his bow and unsheathed a sword from his belt. The bow limbs bent, and the fistmele spun and filled into a green-painted round shield.

"Asgeir," he said.

"Ullr, you've come to me in my dream," Asgeir said in awe.

"Remember how your brother died, and you will live."

Ullr lunged forward, raised his shield, and swung the sword just a hair's length from Asgeir's eye, then he lunged forward again, thrusting the sword into the air an ell's length.

"But that's Ulf's technique," Asgeir said.

"Heed what I say."

Ullr, now shod with wooden skis bound around his booted feet, skied away, and Asgeir found himself back on Holm. He went to place his hand on his brother's shoulder, but his brother brushed it away. Ulf stood there, his teeth bared like some beast of prey.

"How could you," Asgeir's mother said with a sob, "I raised my boy better than that!"

Sakka stood before his mother, swollen-bellied. Meanwhile, Ulf chomped down like Nosey on Arild. Asgeir walked toward them both, Gael-Kisser in hand.

After that dream, he had another night of dreamless sleep. At dawn, the he-thralls fetched Asgeir. Neither Frida nor Arild had come to visit then, just the thralls to feed him. One of the thralls had mentioned that Arild's finger had turned green and black and he had traveled to Borgund, further inland, to Jarl Haakon there, who kept a doctor in his court. His mother went with him, so Asgeir had a quiet few days. His legs felt heavy and his back sore as he stepped out into the open for the first time in days. His eye had opened again, and his headaches eased, but his wounds still harried him. *I hurt, yet I must duel still. Luckily, Arild has a worse injury.*

A rancid he-thrall took Asgeir down to the little boat, carrying him over his shoulders like a sack of flour. Asgeir cringed against the back of his slimy neck. When they came to the riverbank, the thrall set him down. Asgeir stumbled around like a newborn lamb. The thrall left him, and he found two familiar faces sitting in the boat.

Njall and Foul-Farter waved from the boat, along with Erle who looked eager to row. Foul-Farter said something terse, and the three of them laughed as Njall waved in Asgeir.

Asgeir raised his head skyward. *Thank Thor, defender of man. From one captor to these unruly vikings, perhaps, but these are preferable.*

"I'm just happy I can walk," he said to them as he stretched his legs like a cat getting up from a nap, and nearly stumbled into the bow of the boat.

The fat, hairy Foul-Farter bear-hugged him.

"Good to see you alive!"

Njall reached up and ruffled Asgeir's hair, his cheeks even more wrinkled as he grinned. "That piece of shit with the bow—we got out of there by the skin of our balls!"

Asgeir found himself smirking when he thought of Sakka, as he remembered her coos.

"We," Foul-Farter said, and then laughed, his belly jutting out under the pole of his oar. "We heard what you did! All of Laerdal has, thanks to Frida's gossipy tongue!"

The men's laughter echoed throughout the dell. Asgeir flushed.

"How'd you all fare?" he asked.

"Good you distracted Arild when Ulf, Rolf, and Sveinn were stuck in those traps," Njall said. "After he got the snake off him, I rushed him with a stick. Rolf climbed up and got his father out. When he saw the look on Ulf's face, that hunter screamed like a girl and ran off. Bah! So much injustice in this valley. We're sacrificing highly to Tyr today," Njall said, "though if that was really his wife, what more could be meted out?"

"His wife-to-be."

Njall laughed. "Still!"

The youthful sailor prodded the riverbed with his oar and sent the boat adrift, and they rowed west, toward Bjorkum.

Asgeir and the crew arrived at the camp still in the early morning. They rowed past the beached Sea-Bitch. *I never thought I'd be happy to see that sight.* The dragon figurehead seemed to roar him a welcome, and Svartganger popped his little black head over the rail and meowed silently.

Svartganger!

Ulf's thralls had been cooking breakfast, including Éabhín, rolling dough on a flat board. She glanced up at him, blushed, and continued rolling.

Erle docked the boat, and they all went ashore. Ulf emerged from the ship in a long, unblemished linen tunic, stretched, and yawned as he walked down the gangway.

The old man frowned at him, but there had been laughter in his eyes, and Asgeir nearly shivered at that.

"You've gotten into trouble, lad."

"And you, uninjured?" he asked.

Ulf nodded. "Thank Thor my son was safe. If that scoundrel had hurt him, I would send him to the snake-pit like Ragnar. That idiot son of Rudolf High-Hat," and he laughed now, but frowned, "you avenged us good in the bed of Arild's girl. No more to be said, lad. Go get cleaned up and dressed. And bring something to sacrifice to Tyr."

"I don't have anything, I hardly brought anything with me."

"The cat?" Ulf said with a laugh, but then shook his head. "No, that's the ship's mouser. You'll make sense of it." He stole off over to his tent and disappeared through the flaps of the canvas.

Éabhín glanced at Asgeir, her arms powdery up to her elbows. He went over to her, but she waved her hand under her nose.

"You smell funny," she said and turned away, sour-faced.

"Better clean yourself up, or you'll smell like Sveinn," Njall said. "Hurry up—we sacrifice to Tyr soon!"

Asgeir went to bathe in the river, and after he had cleaned himself, the sky lightened. On the ship, he petted Svartganger for a long while, and then dressed himself. He pinned his cloak with the silver brooch that Ulf had given him. Rolf, still in his linen undertunic and britches, approached.

"Good to see you alive," Rolf said, "we thought you had perished up in the mountains."

"I may perish at the Thing," he said with a grin and a forced laugh.

"Perish? What do you mean?"

"I'm to challenge Arild, the son of Frida, to a duel."

"You too," he said. "I'm to duel Arild."

Rolf swallowed his last bite of the cheese. "Duel Arild?"

"I caught him off-guard and had a knife to his throat. I told him he would duel me to settle our quarrel. He agreed, even swore to it. I'm tired of all this murder, plotting, and banditry."

"My friend, you aren't so good at dueling."

"I'll defeat him," Asgeir said, and for an eyeblink, he remembered the way Rolf whirled his shield about during the duel on Holm.

Rolf raised his eyebrows. "Well, you will sacrifice something to Tyr, will you not?"

"I don't know what," he said. "I ought to sacrifice this brooch—I don't want to be Ulf's man. Everyone will know I'm his little puppy dog as long as I wear it."

Rolf clenched his jaw, but then said, "I guess I would be angry too if I had to wear the brooch of someone who killed my brother. But you can't sacrifice that."

"What's Ulf going to do, kill me?"

"No," Rolf said, "man, think about it. It's a sacrifice. It's something you want, something you love. Do you love that brooch?"

"Of course not."

"Will you miss it?"

"No, I want to trade it as soon as I can."

"Sacrifice something you will miss after it's gone."

Rolf reached into a nearby satchel and showed Asgeir a block of yellow cheese. "Hungry?"

The two sat on a chest and nibbled at the cheese for a while.

"What ill luck," Rolf said, "that we were waylaid by the son of that cunt."

"The Norns spun something weird. I've become tangled up in it."

"We all have," Rolf said, "but we survived thus far. I thought we were going to die in that elk-trap. Luckily you distracted him long enough for us to get out."

They both fell silent for a spell.

"Well, thank you, Asgeir. And good to have you back."

A sailor called out to Rolf. He stood up, nodded to Asgeir, and left.

A girl's voice piped up in Gaelic from behind him.

"I'm happy to see you home," Éabhín said.

"Home?" Asgeir said. "That makes me sick. Why would you say that?"

Éabhín groaned. "Do you deny it?"

"What?"

"This ship's your home."

"I admit, I was so happy to see the Sea-Bitch after I had been up in the mountains. And a few nights ago, I slept in a cave."

"No, you slept in some girl's bed!" she said, red-faced.

"What's it to you?" he asked.

"Nothing," she said. "I'm just telling you, this ship is your home."

"It's your home then, too."

"Only until they find out that I'm no slave," she said and she shook her head. "Once they find that out, they'll be real sorry. Your eye is better, but your face looks even worse. You're all bruised up!"

His nose pulsed. He ran a finger along his eyebrow that had been raised as his face swelled up.

"I've been through a lot these last few nights," he said, "I am in want of comfort, not thorns, if that is all you offer."

She frowned hard. "You're real dirty! You know that? I heard the sailors talking 'bout what you did with that Finngirl. That is... disgusting! She's not your wife!"

"What's it to you?" he asked.

"It's nothing to me," she said as she looked at her bare feet. "I just liked having someone to speak Gaelic to, and you ran off with some slut!"

"Ran off?" he said. "Don't you know what I've been through? I was nearly killed!"

"Nearly killed, so you go and hump the first thing you see, like a horny dog?"

"She's a Finn, she's heading back north."

"Yeah? I overheard that the Finns are coming back down from the mountains. Good for Ulf and his crew so they can get that tar. That makes you happy, huh?"

"Slave girl!" Ulf shouted from the beach. "Get up here and work!"

Éabhín reddened, bit her lip, and shook her hair about her face.

"They'll be real sorry," she said as she climbed down the ladder of the hull of the ship.

He thought back to her on the riverside, after he had saved her from a watery grave. *Ran's realm. Just who was she, if she was not supposed to be a slave?*

Asgeir swallowed the last of the cheese. *That was nice of Rolf, can't say I fault him for much. What will he do after I slay his father? I guess I don't know what is spun for us.*

The dream he had of Ullr came to him. Sword in the eye...

No, I must think of Tyr now. I must sacrifice something I love for him, so I may win justly against Arild. That will settle it all. He gazed back up at the white-gray mantle of the mountains.

I miss you, Sakka. I wonder if I'll see you again. Maybe you will sacrifice to your bear god to protect me.

But what to sacrifice to Tyr?

Rolf was right. He must give something to the gods that he cherished. The brooch Ulf had given Asgeir bound him like an oathsman. It glimmered at his shoulder, but he valued it as just scrap silver. He ought to trade it after he freed himself from Ulf's yoke. It meant nothing, so the gods would not see it fit for sacrifice. *But what could I give up then?*

Besides Svartganger, who trilled as Asgeir rubbed his belly, nothing else mattered much. He'd left behind his dear possessions when he set forth as a crewman of the Sea-Bitch. He felt strangely fond of his stool, despite sitting on it just for a day, but he needed it to prop his ass up as he rowed. He had left his finely woven clothes back at his farm and, of course, Ulf still had Gael-Kisser.

Looking over his body, he just found his winingas to be worthwhile. They were spun by his mother in herringbone twill from the South Isles, and braided garters held them fast by brass hooks. They kept his legs warm, they warded against briars and bugbites, and they kept his trousers from snagging things. Odd had worn a pair just like them. He had found his sacrifice.

The glassy pond lapped at the soggy ground between the plowed field and the cliffside. Ulf sat horsed in his red cloak over his chain shirt. All the oarsmen of the Sea-Bitch stood there with him, each also in their red cloaks pinned with silver brooches, in a half-circle around the pond. Each held something close to their chests. Asgeir stood at the opposite end of Ulf, his two winingas wound up in rolls and clutched against his chest.

"Today, we honor Tyr, the most righteous among the Aesir, who knowingly lost his hand to bind the wolf Fenris. Tyr granted me two victories this week: against Ketill Redcloak and against the two Norse-Gael brothers in holmgang."

Asgeir's breath stopped as he found himself back on the island, Odd's quaking body on the strand, his winingas-wrapped legs twitching. He eyed Ulf, and Ulf returned his gaze. *Ulf knows I hate him. But he knows I will only kill him in a fair fight, under the guidance of my father.*

"Now I call upon you for a third victory," Ulf said. "Grant us a victory at your hunting-ground, the Thing, where unjust cretins have befouled your right hand through lies, treachery, and zest for murder. For this, we sacrifice to you, but first..." He cleared his throat and sang:

I know your hand guides mine,

Aesir of most honor high.

Honor is our strong twine,

Under your righteous blue sky.

The wolf Fenris is bound,

Your severed hand to the ground.

To you our hard-earned things,

For always justice you sing.

Ulf snatched a pouch from his belt, the leather thong snapped, and he chucked it into the pond, the silver coins within the pouch jangling in the air as it plummeted.

"For Tyr," Sveinn said, and tossed an antler-carved comb in next.

"Tyr will avenge us by his severed hand," Njall Gray-Hair said as he tossed a handful of glass beads that cascaded into the water.

"For Tyr, and for justice, my mother's knife," Rolf said, and first threw a brass-adorned leather sheath, and then flung a bone-handled knife in with it.

"For Tyr, my winingas," Asgeir said, but Ulf said, "No."

Asgeir looked up at him as the old captain rummaged through a saddlebag. *What's his deal? And it's my sacrifice.*

He tossed something to Asgeir, and he found himself holding a cloudberry-colored cloak, dyed in the same color as the rest of the men there.

"Who made your cloak?"

"My mother."

"Of course. Sacrifice your cloak, put the new one on, and keep your winingas. It will get cold on the boat when we cross the North Sea. You need them."

What a brilliant color! This must be madder, from the Mediterranean. My father would be proud to see me donned in this. I'm almost happy to wear Ulf's style of cloak. He rewrapped his legs with the winingas and unbrooched his cloak.

"Tyr, I sacrifice this cloak to you," he said as the breeze blew colder across his unprotected tunic. He held the cloak aloft as it fluttered in the breeze, and then tossed it into the pond.

Rolf took Asgeir's new, scarlet-red garment from Ulf's hands and spread it. Asgeir hesitated to take it, but Rolf looked nearly giddy. *Did he want me to wear the same cloak as them?*

Bunching up the cloak over his right shoulder, he pierced it with its silver pin and cinched it. All fell silent for a spell, but Rolf cheered and clapped, as did Ulf and Njall. Soon, the other sailors joined them, and they thronged around them.

Asgeir stood there at Tyr's pond, cloaked like them, broached like them, and Ulf belted his song to Tyr again. The sailors sang along with him, one after the other in a roll, and after the third verse, Asgeir joined and sang along at the top of his lungs.

The freemen of Laerdal all came down to the Thing. The last Thing of the year, the Leid, occurred along with the harvest and the final slaughter, where the hundred freemen would venture to settle all disputes and legalities of the year. All of the freemen would moot there that morning to settle all the week's quarrels by wapentake, the vote by noise of weapon.

Twenty-seven freemen went out to the Thing-farm by horse or boat to the flat land. There, the land jutted out much like a knuckle, where one could speak downwind to cast one's voice and all could hear. Low cairns and mounds of the anonymous alderelders rested there. The dead had soil heaped upon them to mark the land as one to revere, to watch, and to guard against injustices and ill will. Justice reigned at the Thing, the god Tyr himself had been called upon and named in sacrifice, and all had to obey this elder call for righteous behavior.

Asgeir stood with Rolf, Njall, and Sveinn, all cloaked, at the bow of the Sea-Bitch. The freemen gathered within the roped-off circle at the foot of the speaking-hill. They awaited the lawman, armed with spears and shields, though a few of the richest ones walked with swords from their belts.

Ulf stood midships, horsed.

"I'm confident the lawman will side with me. Rudolf High-Hat's wife is treacherous and conniving, but also arrogant, and that'll do her in. As for you, it's not going to be easy to defend you with a straight face," Ulf said to Asgeir. "That Svear woman and her murderous son got what was coming to them when you slew the maidenhood of his bride-to-be. I'm sure her hotness and wetness was worth whatever penalty they'll lob at you! Maybe you'll end up with a wife—either way, Arild will cry."

A ship with a wide, bright-red sail floated over the river from the east in the morning light. Dozens of oars waited as the ship steered toward the landing-point. A dragon-head rode the prow like that of the Sea-Bitch, but painted red, a yawning drakkar of the Jarl Haakon of Borgund. Thralls at the landing place helped drag it up as men disembarked, some with swords in scabbards strapped to their belts. The crew of the Sea-Bitch disembarked and joined the crowd on the sward.

Asgeir found Frida among some red-cloaked freemen. She waited cross-armed over her blue coat. She must have been there to vote in the stead of her husband.

Jarl Haakon came down the ramp of the ship horsed on a white stallion with a blond mane. The horse's bit was brass, but shone like gold in the sun. The jarl wore a strawberry-red cloak like Ketill's, but bloodier scarlet and bordered in sallow-colored silk.

When the horseman passed, the trappings of his rider-gear rung like bells, and Asgeir saw his hat was lined with yellow silk thread. A silver armband flashed from his upper arm, and he had a short-cropped gray beard. As he walked past Ulf, he paid him no mind. When he trudged upland and to the Thing moot, he carried on as the crowd parted. They cheered him as he rode into the center of the ring, dismounted, unsheathed a sword, and held it aloft.

A he-thrall came and led his horse away as the crowd gathered around him. The jarl trudged up the hill and spoke to the freemen below.

"My warriors, my friends, my kin," Jarl Haakon said through a wooden loudhailer, "today we moot to solve misdeeds, and avoid further misfortune than that which has already befallen our peaceful dale. We call forth firstly an outlander called Ulf the Old."

The old warrior swung his leg over his horse and dismounted.

Éabhín led Ulf's horse away by the reins.

"You may even end up as a father!" she said, and three nearby sailors stifled laughter.

"I am here to bring Tyr's just hand to this valley, mired in treachery," Ulf said.

Asgeir turned to find that by some boulders, some colorfully dressed men stood: Finnmen in their red-yellow tunics. Sakka's father eyed him from underneath a green-and-white striped hood. Behind him, a girl in a heather-yellow dress lowered her gaze and hid behind him: Sakka.

He wanted to hug her against him, cradle her, and kiss her. But he could not. *Would I ever again?*

"Finnmen?" said Erle, behind Asgeir, his face loosened into a nonplussed expression. "A Finn?"

"What?"

"The Finnman father will hex you, each beat of his Finn-drum a hex from Hel."

"Hail the day of justice," Jarl Haakon spoke down to the freemen.

"Free men—Thor's children," the jarl said, "all shall know the laws of the land!"

Jarl Haakon recounted the law, which had come down from Odin when he first whelped jarl, karl, and thrall upon Midgard, and told how men ought to and ought to not act, and what price they must pay for lawlessness. When that had been done, the jarl continued.

"Today, I, Lawspeaker Jarl Haakon, have been asked to call the Thing early. This unusual occurrence is due to the presence of some guests visiting the market, who ended up raiding and killing my huskarl, Ketill Redcloak, because, allegedly, Gro had plotted with Frida Two-Plaits, wife of Rudolf High-Hat, who represents her husband here at the Thing today, for he has been banished for nine winters.

"Ketill's death was an honorable one. Ulf the Old and his sailors attacked his home in daylight, eager for an honorable battle and were met by the warriors of Ketill, and indeed, the valkyries flew over Rikheim that day, for Ulf the Old had wanted a fair fight, as witnessed by the survivors of the raid. The feud between Ulf the Old and Ketill Redcloak was settled by blood, and as peace-weaver, I shall seek no other retribution for the slayings of my huskarl and his men, by Freyr, god of peace."

Ulf half-smirked.

"Yet he alleges that Frida, a member of our Thing in the stead of her husband, had plotted his murder by poison. And too, Gro of the Rocky-Bend, who Ulf had put to death, was also allegedly involved. The witness to this murder plot is Asgeir, son of the Gael-Slayer, in-debt to Ulf the Old as a sailor.

"Next, Ulf the Old, Njall Gray-Hair, Sveinn Foul-Farter, and Rolf Ulfsson allege that the son of Frida and Rudolf High-Hat's son, Arild Rudolfsson, had attempted to murder them up the mountain. And peculiarly, Asgeir escaped, only to be captured by Arild some hours later. Then, while Arild was away, Asgeir had bedded his bride-to-be, the Finngirl Sakka, and now both Arild and the Finnman, Gealbu from Finnmark, wish for compensation.

"Without a doubt, we all wish we could wait until Leid to settle the score, but neither Ulf nor Gealbu and his company will dwell for another month here and, to avoid more violence, we had to confer here today, ignore our daily duties, and disturb our peace. For that, I must say, all parties involved have acted as vikings and buffoons, and I am ashamed to say that I share kinship with any of them."

Some in the crowd chuckled. Frida crossed her arms tighter.

"Firstly, we call up Asgeir, son of Hallgeir the Gael-Slayer. He will bear witness to what he heard on the farm where Gro of the Rocky Bend and Frida Two-Plait allegedly plotted to murder Ulf by nightshade."

Asgeir crossed the rope and stood in the center of the freemen. His body quaked; all eyes lay upon him, and he struggled to utter his first word.

"I overheard her speaking at Gro's farm," Asgeir said, "discussing Ulf the Old, my captain. First, they were to bring Frida's daughter to Bjorkum at the market and woo Ulf, and invite him to Frida's farm for dinner that night to discuss a possible marriage. When Ulf was to arrive, they would poison his drink."

Gasps rippled through the crowd.

"The rest of you men—Ulf the Old, Njall Gray-Hair, Rolf Ulfsson, and Sveinn Foul-Farter, you are all witnesses—has Asgeir spoken the truth?"

The four men nodded.

"That's five witnesses for one story. What say you in your defense, Lady Frida?"

Frida walked forward, her neat plaits flopping over her shoulders as she came into the circle.

"I am afraid that the son of Hallgeir the Gael-Slayer lies. Did you know what he did three nights ago? He bedded Sakka of the Finns—the bride-to-be of my boy! Yes, you heard that right—a bastard may roll from between the legs of my future daughter-in-law! If he would do such a dreadful thing, then why would he not lie?

"I for one believe that Ulf the Old wanted an excuse to raid and kill Ketill! He wished to fill his coffer before he voyaged out to Hjaltland, and what better way than a raid here in our very Laerdal?

"We had peace, we had not had even so much a squabble that led into a duel for generations. Yet Ulf the Old shows up, and the very same day, a farm is raided and the jarl's huskarl is murdered?

"Let us not forget who this Ulf the Old is. He rode right into Bjorkum carrying the scalp of poor Ketill—and even a woman, our dear friend Gro, had not been spared by his swordsmen—what sort of monster would commit such a misdeed? He could not even give peace to his perceived enemy in death, let alone to our valley!

"He undoubtedly put up this Asgeir to lying. Unlike Ulf, Asgeir comes from a noble tree, that of Hallgeir the Gael-Slayer, huskarl of the King of Lothlend. Son, please, come forward and admit that you are lying, and Ulf had forced you to! If you do, you may be spared punishment!"

Asgeir stood as still as a ship beached at low tide.

She turned back to Jarl Haakon upon the hillock. "I know that, for a fact, Ulf took this lad from his home after slaying his brother in a duel and, much to the ire of this boy, forced him aboard his ship. You may ask why would this boy lie to save that scoundrel's life? The answer is simple: Ulf would kill him if he didn't!

"Shall that excuse Asgeir of his crime against the maidenhood of my future daughter-in-law, and the dishonoring and maiming of my poor son? No, these were affronts to Freyja her very self—but this first charge? Clearly, he was not responsible for his actions, no more than a thrall can be sentenced for carrying out the will of his master."

Rolf was right to call her a cunt.

"I am not lying," Asgeir said. "And I will not lie when I say that I hate Ulf. I hate him for what he did to my brother, and I hate him for what he did to my family, but no one deserves to die by poison." Asgeir nearly said, *except for you,* but held his tongue. "And someday, I will kill him, but in honorable single combat, allowed by the King of Lothlend, if Tyr loves me, and not by your little sniveling plot."

Ulf, expressionless, nodded at Asgeir.

"Lawman, allow me to address this Asgeir."

"You've spoken your piece," Haakon said.

They left the circle, and Haakon raised the loudhailer.

"I, the lawspeaker, now wish to remind the freemen that the penalty for plotting death is banishment. Now, is Frida guilty? Wapentake!"

Men beat their spearshafts against their shield faces. Asgeir counted—one, two, three, nine, ten… eighteen! *More than half!*

Frida never ceased her sneer, but she folded her arms tight over her chest and stood silent.

"The freemen of Laerdal have spoken. I then sentence Frida Two-Plait to banishment to Orkney. May she join her husband there. If she cannot afford the voyage, she will have to sell her possessions to do so. She must leave before summer's end. And may I remind her that it is near."

Arild shouted something nearby, but it was garbled and Asgeir couldn't hear it much over the beating of the shields from the wapentake. The Svear lady huffed but stood her ground, ready to wapentake for the next case.

"Just banishment?" Ulf asked Njall, the latter shaking his head. "She was the cause of all of this!"

"Next we call Arild Rudolfsson," he said. "Come forward, lad."

Arild approached, his right hand bandaged. He walked into the circle pointed his forefinger-less hand at Ulf.

"My mother gets banished, but Ulf, who insulted her, gets nothing?"

"You will quiet yourself, for Tyr has crowned me lawspeaker," Haakon said.

"You stand before your neighbors accused of attempting to murder five guests in Laerdal. Ulf the Old, Njall Gray-Hair, Sveinn Foul-Farter, Rolf Ulfsson, and Asgeir, son of the Gael-Slayer. It is alleged that three of the five fell into elk traps, and you were going to murder them all by your arrows. They were saved when Asgeir distracted you, and you chased him into the mountains. There are five witnesses to this. What say you?"

"They are lying," Arild said, "to murder men would be cowardly, and I am no coward. They fell into my elk traps because they didn't see them, and they mistook that I had dug them there to kill them, when I wished to trap elk or deer, and they set upon me. I ran away. If I had meant to murder them, I could have shot one or two before they even saw me coming, for I had been in a hunting-blind, and they did not notice me until they were already in the pits. If I'm lying, then why are they all unscathed? Asgeir attacked me," he said as he held up his still-bandaged arm, "by tossing an adder at me, like a stealthy murderer. I escaped and fled to the shelter of my wife-to-be, and even took Asgeir, lost in the mountains, as a guest in our tent after by happenstance he found us, and he betrayed me."

Haakon gestured to the free farmers. "Then we shall wapentake, of who speaks truth, and who speaks lies…"

Sakka had run toward the ring. "Wait!" she shouted, her twang thick.

Gealbu attempted to grab her, but he caught nothing but the fuzzy threads of her thick cloak as she slipped away and rushed toward the moot.

"No, he is lying!" she pointed at Arild.

Asgeir stood aghast.

Some in the crowd gasped when the Finngirl centered herself in the moot.

Arild frowned and furrowed his brows. No one had called her, and Haakon raised his hand to halt her speech, but she continued.

"He admitted it that he wanted to kill them! He was going to murder Asgeir too until I pleaded for him not to! It was why I felt so much pity for him…" She went red, tears in her dark eyes, and she turned and fled away.

"I had not called this witness," Jarl Haakon said. "I must remind the Finnmen to control their own, yet I know I can never silence her. Freemen, you have heard enough. Wapentake!"

"Wait!" Arild shouted. "Let me say that this is a farce—I have agreed with Asgeir to settle our dispute by the sword. Forget this case—forget about Sakka—good Jarl Haakon, allow me a duel with Asgeir, and we will right it all!"

He's got the battle fury about him—is the time really here? Will I really face him in a duel? Me? The one who lost to Ulf and Rolf so easily?

The crowd gasped and muttered.

"I disagree," Frida said, "let him face Tyr's decree!" Tears appeared in her eyes. "Please! Let us not settle this with weapons—my boy, I cannot bear this! We are better than this, let us settle this with words and laws, not violence!"

"Silence! All silence!" Haakon yelled, and all went silent. The jarl stroked his gray beard three times. "The god of justice, Tyr, decides on this matter. I can feel in my bones that he calls single combat! If both parties agree, then let us ask the freemen—if the sayer of victory may inspire them—what do they think? Yay or nay? Wapentake!"

The men began to beat upon their shields with their spearshafts in a clank. Asgeir counted ten, eleven—twenty-six—all but Frida, who stood there as quiet as bog water.

I am relieved in one way. His heart thudded hard, and he became aware of it. *But can I really defeat Arild?*

"Men—you have decided! Tyr has called for justice! We will allow both combatants to rest and prepare. Asgeir and Arild shall fight today at sundown—let Ullr decide who is the most right, through the blade!"

The men all cheered. Asgeir caught Sakka staring at him, but her father took her arm and led her away toward a pair of tents on the riverside. Frida embraced Arild and sobbed on his shoulder, while Haakon and some of the farmers stood in a cluster, speaking off by the hill.

"You're going through with the duel," Ulf said.

"Yes," Asgeir said, "I was tired of all of this murder, chasing, sneaking business."

"Settle it like men then."

"Yes," Asgeir said. "I want honor."

"You're awful at dueling. Remember our holmgang, when I bested you? Do you even know how to use a sword?"

"I know some things."

"Arild was in Haakon's leidang. He went on a raid in Denmark when you were playing with your cock. You're unlucky—he's only missing one finger. And he has every reason to want to kill you, after you fucked that Finngirl."

Asgeir felt something staring at him. He turned, and it was Éabhín, with a horrid gaze like a blue flame.

"We had him, you fool," Ulf said, "we had them. We heard that they went over to Borgund and licked the jarl's feet, but he had none of it. Arild had fought in his shieldwall, and he still had none of it. Maybe Frida even licked something else, and he still had none of it. All bullshit to the jarl. He could smell a liar, so he was on our side. He would have banished them both. Maybe they would have gone to Iceland, and no one would have to see that awful she-wolf and her stupid son ever again. And what, concern for fucking the girl? Just marry her. She has wide hips—it would have been fine, she would have given you sons apt at reindeer herding. You fool."

Asgeir had to remember to breathe. He gulped.

"Now you may die in a duel against Arild. Even if you survive, we lose, because we could have had him banished, along with his serpent of a mother. You're arrogant, just like your brother. It will undo you. It undid him right through the eye. You fool."

You remind me of that? Asgeir stood there, about to choke, as he wished to remind Ulf that he would face him in single combat someday.

Ulf walked off, grabbing Njall and Rolf by their shoulders. They turned, but Njall approached Asgeir.

I'll show you, Ulf.

For a moment, Asgeir spotted Arild off in the distance. Frida stood there with a sword in her right hand and a shield wedged in her armpit. First with the shield, and then with the sword, Arild armed himself. A swordsman of Jarl Haakon.

He has seen war, and I have not. What am I doing?

"Don't get yourself killed, maybe Thor will help you, like Bride helped me," Éabhín said. "Because of you, I had to call upon that heathen god of the Dubh Linn woods!" she spat on the ground and stomped away from Asgeir.

"We just have a few hours, lad," Njall said as he patted the sword at his belt. "Let's warm up and train some. It's your best chance to win."

Asgeir still stared after Éabhín as she stormed away, back toward Ulf's ship beached on the riverside.

"Are you daft? Forget the Gaelic girl, you've had a prettier girl anyway, and now the only wetness you will find is blood—yours or his. I'll train you hard, and I have the time now, because there's not much else to do."

Asgeir left the Thing with Njall, and they walked back to the Sea-Bitch.

"Ulf," Asgeir called as they passed the captain.

The old sea-wolf grunted.

"I have no sword for the duel. I want Gael-Kisser."

Ulf walked off wordless again, the red-leathered scabbard bobbing along with his gait.

"There's a clearing over there," Njall said. "We can do some swordplay there."

They went over to the clearing. Ulf went over and sat on his chest at the riverside, hands on his knees, eyes closed. "I prayed hard, and I am a man dedicated to the gods. I lived long, and I will live to see Asgeir defeat Arild

Rudolfsson. Please, Ullr, allow the sword of Asgeir to sever the head of the son of such a loathsome woman."

I hate that he prays for me, yet I must need prayers. Fuck, what shall I do?

Asgeir gazed up at the sky, Tyr's farm, where the god rained justice and honor. It had been decided then, and there was little use in complaining, for now he must worship Ullr— the god of the duel— and sacrifice much to him, to vie against the sword of Arild Rudolfsson, and to free himself of his thirst for revenge.

CHAPTER VII

The Duel

The sword weighed heavy in Asgeir's hand. The handle had been too short, for the dwarves guided the smith's hammer to forge each sword for each swordsman, and this sword had been lengthened to Njall's hand. Asgeir's hand spilled over the five-lobed, bronze-plated pommel. It was the sword that killed Odd.

I dislike using this sword, but I have no other. Blast you, Ulf, I should wield my father's sword! But you think I will lose, and you will not want to wield a loser's sword...

Njall, though at least fifty winters old, stood nearly a head shorter than him. The older man had many scars about his brow that he proudly attributed to swordplay. He had another sword in his hand, a single-edge sword with a round iron pommel, loaned from one of the sailors. The grip had been covered in polished antler and was too long for him.

"In my youth, I was a sellsword," he said. "I killed many men with the sword you hold—my father's blade, but I forged the crossguard and pommel myself. What he taught me kept me alive for a while, and maybe it will keep you alive today."

"Where are our shields?"

"We don't need them yet. You have two shields already."

Njall distanced himself from Asgeir.

"Your first shield is your feet. They defend you. They guard you. They keep you alive. Don't believe me? Go on and strike at me."

Asgeir raised the sword and swung it at Njall's shoulder. The short man backstepped, and the sword sliced nothing but air.

"See? The best defense is your feet keeping you from harm. Your second defense is your sword."

The two spent the afternoon in swordplay. Each parry, each swing, each stab: all for the god Ullr.

I think I'm getting better. I must live up to the name of my father, and defeat Arild.

At one point, Ulf, who had been drinking from the river nearby, got up and walked over to them.

"Short men make good swordsmen, since there's less of them to hit," he said with a grin.

"Tall men make good swordsmen, because of their arm's reach," Njall said.

"Then what of me, who is neither tall nor short?" Asgeir asked.

"Each man must figure that out himself," Njall said.

"Step aside if you have no advice," Ulf said and nudged Njall away. "I suppose my sailors need to know proper warcraft. Let me show you then, Asgeir, how I killed your brother."

Right through the eye.

Njall handed Ulf his sword the right way— that is, hilt first and without the oily blemish of a fingerprint. Ulf took his mate's sword.

"Go on and parry this."

Ulf's sword thrust toward Asgeir in a flash. He made a parry with the flat of his blade, a fine one, but Ulf stepped forward, sliding his blade a thumbnail away from Asgeir's right eye. He held it there.

"That's how I killed your brother. My feet. I took one step forward and the sword went with me, and made mincemeat of your brother's eye, and that was it. So Njall is right for once."

For an eyeblink, Ullr from his dream stood before Asgeir in the same pose.

I dreamt that dream, but what did it tell me? If only I could speak to my Auntie.

"Now how could you stop this?"

Asgeir sidestepped to the right as Ulf pushed his blade back.

"Yes. Now how would you counter?"

Asgeir let Ulf's blade slide into his crossguard, where it was the strongest, and wound his arm down, his elbow crooked, and prodded Ulf's chest with the tip.

"Yes. There we are. I'll live to regret training you," Ulf said with a laugh.

I'll make sure if it.

Ulf handed Njall back his sword and went off down the strand back to the ship.

"Now I have taught you all that I know, duel honorably, and Ullr will have you. You will borrow my sword."

At high-noon, they all walked back to the Thing-place.

Ulf and Njall trained me well. By Thor! I feel myself readied to duel Arild. Right through the eye... Odd, I hate that I know this technique, but may it serve me well.

The ropes had been raised taut to circle the moot place. Jarl Haakon stood upon the hillock to lawspeak. Throngs stood clustered around the circle, not just freemen, but women, children, thralls, their dogs and horses. The breeze blew cold, and something crowed as it flew over the dueling-field.

A hooded crow cawed loud as it ringed about, floated overhead, and flapped eastward until it vanished in the green meld of the forested mountain.

Many in the crowd muttered, until Jarl Haakon spoke.

"My friends," he said, "we hope that both duelists will live, and just the first cut will settle this dispute. But I cannot deny that the crow's flight might have been a sign that Odin himself may have declared death this day."

Whispers and murmurs continued as Asgeir headed through the crowd, many eyes on him as he stepped over the rope and into the ring.

There, at the onset of twilight, Asgeir stood, Njall's sword at his belt.

He wore the cloak and brooch Ulf gifted him. He wished for neither the cloak nor the brooch, but a man never should arrive to a duel underdressed.

Arild came now on his horse with his elkhound at his side. He dismounted with a smirk. The same woad-dyed cloak that his mother wore adorned his shoulders. He wore a silver brooch with two dragon heads, the symbol of Jarl Haakon.

Astride his horse, he petted his mount as Raggi the Elkhound, unscathed, danced about. The hunter pointed a finger heavenward and called out, "Tyr!" In a sweep, he lunged forward, unsheathed his sword, and struck in an arc. He then pointed toward Asgeir and ran his thumb left to right across his own throat.

As he entered the ring, he held up his bandaged hand.

"I earned my brooch, cloak, and sword as the swordsman of Jarl Haakon. He watches me today. I will not falter."

A cloaked girl came up behind the hunter and handed him his shield. It was Sakka, and both of them averted their eyes from the other.

If only Sakka would bring me my weaponry! Arild, I should never feel jealousy for you, but I do now.

Ulf marched over across the sward of the moot place, his long-legged stomp obvious. He thrust a shield forward at Asgeir, handle first. "You forgot this!" he said loudly.

Some in the crowd laughed at Asgeir. Arild tossed his lime-dyed curly hair over his shoulder and grinned.

Asgeir hunched his shoulders. *How embarrassing... Help me, Tyr, to right these wrongs through my sword.*

"The quarrel will be settled now," Haakon said, "by means of a duel. Tyr's justice calls upon Ullr to decide who is right and wrong, because he sides with the bravest man in battle."

Arild Rudolfsson walked forward. He held his blade with the hammer-grip— that is, like one would hammer a nail. Asgeir knew that to be hard-striking, with beats in rhythm. He too held the sword in the hammer-grip, for Arild could not hold it with finesse, for he had lost a finger to Nosey's snout, and honor demanded that he match his stance.

The two approached one another. Njall's words filled Asgeir's mind. His feet both his offense and defense, his sword the second shield, his shield the second sword.

Arild relaxed his right arm and rested his blade behind his back. He approached Asgeir shield-first. Asgeir's breath shortened as he could not see his enemy's sword. He could not predict if it would strike him upward or downward or sideways. But then the gray blade flashed.

Asgeir blocked with his shield, and Arild's blade bounced off the boss, then upward at Asgeir's head. The lad backstepped and caught the blade against the edge of the shield.

Arild tore the blade free. Asgeir saw it had cleft through the rawhide and into the wood of the shield. Arild backed off, and the two squared off again.

Your shield is your third shield...

Asgeir swung his body as he attempted to strike Arild from the side. His sword snapped forward. Arild parried with his own sword and struck at Asgeir. Asgeir leapt back, then darted in again, and when Arild raised his sword to parry, Asgeir thrust his shield forward and smashed through Arild's blade and right toward his face. Arild pivoted away, but Asgeir struck with his sword in a punch with a flip of his wrist over Arild's shield.

Ullr, I honor you with each strike. The duel is your game, swordplay is your rite, to the victor go your spoils. And may I fight as good my father.

Arild parried with his blade, the two swords stood athwart the other and both skyward, and Asgeir lunged forward.

The crowd gasped as Asgeir's sword plunged into Arild's eye. In that moment, he saw again his brother on the island, sword through the eye and deep into the head. Asgeir halted his thrust as Arild stood frozen, the sword tip in his eye. The brooch of Ulf glistened while his brother wheezed. But it was Arild there, and Asgeir refused to press the sword-point into his brain.

Gingerly, he drew Njall's sword from Arild's head. His red eyeball dangled and slid down his tunic landed in the grass. Arild held his bleeding socket, wordless. A shriek erupted from the crowd, and Frida ran over to him. Others crossed the rope and gathered around the defeated, bleeding Arild.

"Thank you, Njall," Asgeir called, not knowing where the first mate stood, "thank you Ullr, and thank you, Tyr. The victory is yours."

And thank you, Ulf.

Asgeir wiped a trickle of blood and goo off Njall's sword on the grass and then sheathed it. He found himself again back on Holm, his brother lying there dead as the rough white waves lapped at the rocky shoulder of the island. Instead, men stood with torches in the darkening sky around them.

"I'm—fine—mother—I—fare—well," Arild said in short bursts.

"Please, remove your hand from your eye!" Frida cried. "Oh, your poor eye, oh!"

"I said I am alright, mother!"

A sudden burst of men raced onto the sward toward Asgeir. Foul-Farter led the charge, his arms outstretched like a child in play, and Ulf's crew flew into Asgeir, a wide many-armed hug. Rolf kissed him on the head, and the sailors all shouted and cheered thrice. A burly sailor grasped Asgeir under his arms and hoisted him up, and the sailors chanted:

Asgeir!

Asgeir!

Asgeir!

He found himself on top of them, hoisted high in the air. His hat slid off his head, and the wind drifted up the skirt of his tunic. He spotted Ulf there on the sidelines, a yellow-toothed grin on his face.

The sailors of the Sea-Bitch set him down and, one by one, they hugged him. Njall squeezed him the hardest. "You really listened to me! You fucking bastard! You won! What swordsmanship!"

Asgeir laughed, but turned again to Ulf, who now nodded. Asgeir mimed the technique he had shown him—thrust the sword forward.

"Ullr decrees that it is all settled," Jarl Haakon said through the loudhailer. "Asgeir has found victory. May neither Asgeir, son of the Gael-Slayer, nor Arild Rudolfsson ever quarrel again, and may Ullr step aside in Laerdal and welcome Freyr, god of peace."

"By Freyr, by Ullr, by Tyr— how has this been settled? My son is maimed!" Frida said, a sob in her voice. All at once she came forward with Sakka's parents, both in thick hoods and foul frowns.

Jarl Haakon had come down from his hillock and stood just three men apart from them now.

Arild whined as he sat on the sward. An elderly woman had waddled over and dabbed his eye with a cloth, and she went about prodding and poking at him while humming to herself.

"Asgeir defeated him," Haakon said.

"And my son is expected to marry that harlot?" she said, arms thrown wide in disbelief.

Gealbu turned red, but his wife took his arm and urged him away.

"Again, all must be well in our valley."

"I am outlawed, my son forced to marry a cheater—my daughter-in-law may birth a bastard—what god decides this travesty of law?"

"It is final."

Frida's two he-thralls propped Arild up and carried the hunter away while the elderly woman approached to fix and heal him. Frida turned and glared at Haakon.

"My son is not going to marry her! The son of the Gael-Slayer made his wife there in the Finn's tent, and it will not be my son tied to her unmade bed for the rest of his life!"

She huffed and walked off, calling the name of her son with a wavering voice.

Gealbu glared at Asgeir.

"Wait," Asgeir said, "forget our fight! I'm willing to see your daughter again!"

The Finnman motioned with his arms in the manner of beating a drum. His wife grasped his shoulders to pull him away, and they blended into the crowd.

Asgeir shuddered at that, for the Finns could inflict a hex with their drums.

"But tell Sakka I miss her!" he shouted.

Ulf walked to Asgeir.

"Did the impossible and made him more handsome," he said, and laughed. "More Odinic. By the gods, lad, I thought you were dead."

"Your advice saved me," Asgeir said, and smiled. "I ought to owe you some thanks."

"I suppose I undervalued your skill," Ulf said. "But that Svear harridan will be back like flies on shit, so keep your wits about you. It won't be over until their tree is uprooted and thrown over to Iceland."

Jarl Haakon approached them, his bare hands outstretched.

"Friends," he said, "the evening is young. I would like to invite you sailors to Borgund to my hall, where we will feast, for we have no more quarrels. Come, board your ship and we sail to my hall—it is high tide now, and night is upon us."

Ulf walked off with Haakon, trailed by their armsmen and sailors. The night grew chilly, and the roar of the crowd calmed into a chatter of the birds from the trees.

The flecks of blood on the grass reminded Asgeir again of Odd's death. Did he suffer from lingering so long? His funeral would be soon, and Asgeir had no time to attend. He had to follow Ulf, row on his ship, swab the deck, scrape barnacles off the hull, get into trysts with Finngirls...

He found himself back at the moot, with just some stragglers left. The crew of the Sea-Bitch had been boarding the ship, and they would holler for him soon.

Asgeir fingered the hilt of Njall's sword. He thought to tell his father all about this. His father walked the world as a viking. He had been skilled in the duel circle and a renowned swordsman. Would his father have been proud? Asgeir had fought with honor, but what if he had died? His father would have had no sons, no more odalmenn. His mother perhaps would have died of grief.

Yet he had won.

"Come on! You glorious little shit!" Njall called from the gangway of the Sea-Bitch. "Hurry yourself up, we eat good tonight!"

The hooded crow returned, wheeling overhead. It let out a single caw and landed nearby, pecking about the grass. Hungry for gore. That poor crow, he had not gotten the chance to flense Arild's eye, since it had been plucked up by Frida, as if it could be reattached.

I'm happy he lives, but I fear he may yet cause me trouble. This crow might be telling me that—it may be a sign.

He boarded the ship, and the Sea-Bitch sailed up the river as night fell, eastward, to the mead-hall of Borgund.

CHAPTER VIII

The God of Spears

The hall of Borgund stood just by the river on a raised hill crowned in stone ramparts: the fortified hillfort of Jarl Haakon. The boat-shaped building had wooden tiles with dragon heads roaring from the roof of its north and south ends. The dragon was evil, for the dragon would kill Thor someday, so man ought to honor dragons to ward wickedness from his home. The hall was so long and tall that Asgeir found himself like a babe at his mother's bosom. He had only seen a hall that size and that glamorous down at Karmoy, the hall of the Sea-King that taxed the southernmost end of the North-Way.

Haakon greeted them at the ingang, two stout doors carved with stealthy faces and interlocked beasts with an iron knocker. Inside, the long-hearth blazed high, and Asgeir's eyes stung from the fire of the great smoke that funneled out of the chimney in the roof. The hall stood five men high, and thick oak trunk-posts and overhanging beams held it all together.

The jarl's company stood at the ready inside the hall, gathered on benches around the long-fire. Chief among them, a skald played a lyre with a shining amber bridge. As Ulf's sailors marched through the stone-paved ingang, the skald came to the end of a song, and stopped to tune the strings with a peg. A long-table had been spread with a bleached, fine-linen tablecloth, with plates of alder and a soapstone cup for each of them. Shields and spears garnished the walls, and an oak table stood in front of a wooden seat that was raised high off the floor. A barrel of mead stood nearby, and a lofty woman— the jarl's wife, Saga,— tall with a marble chin, stood in her silk-lined red dress, ladle in hand.

Jarl Haakon beckoned Ulf the Old and his crew over to the barrel, which emitted the sweetest scent of mead with a pinch of elderflower. Haakon and Ulf grasped each other's forearms, and the jarl said:

"I, Haakon, son of Haavard, and a grandson of Odin under the guise of Rig, have called this feast in honor of Freyr, god of peace. May he bring peace and plenty upon our valley, and end these quarrelsome days. May Odin, my first father, guide king Harald, who promises to put an end to this viking business once and for all. Now come, dear guests, tonight we drink the mead of Odin."

He raised a brass-rimmed drinking horn and handed it to his wife. Saga dunked the horn into the mead and filled it, and Haakon drank the first draft. The men filling the hall cheered, and the sailors waited in rows to receive their drink. Ulf was first, and he gulped his horn full down in one draft. He handed the empty horn back to Saga. One by one, the sailors of the Sea-Bitch drank from the horn. As they did, the skald, a blond man with a snubbed nose, played his lyre, and he sang not in Norse, but Gaelic

> *The days have grown old,*
>
> *The swords swing untold,*
>
> *Without a yarn for the Norn to spin,*
>
> *Many sea-wolves alight a din.*
>
> *The sea-horses trample asunder,*
>
> *When men seek only plunder.*

The skald strummed the lyre as the flames danced behind his moss-green tunic. He wore a dragon-headed bronze brooch pinned at the shoulder, the sign of Haakon, but his cloak had been wrapped around him many times, and his legs were bare. Asgeir knew this manner of dress as the fashion of the Gaels of Ireland, and the South Isles that lay on the seaway between Ireland and Norway.

"What a beautiful voice," Njall said. "It's too bad he sings in his own tongue, so who fucking knows what he sings."

"It's Gaelic," Asgeir said.

"Yes, that is Odharnait, after all. He was a bard over there on his island, before the vikings came. Now he plays for Jarl Haakon, who finds the Gaelic tongue alluring."

A warmth spilled over Asgeir. *I could hug him!*

Odharnait plucked the lyre daintily, notes fluttering up and melding with the crackle of the hearth.

Asgeir walked over to him and raised a hand.

"I'm Asgeir," he said in Gaelic, "and I like your song."

The skald stood taken aback, though he continued to strum. "I didn't expect to hear my tongue," he said back in Gaelic, "from someone dressed as a Norseman. Forgive me, Asgeir. I am Odharnait of Barrøy."

"That's in the South Islands."

"Aye. It's a wee island, where a jarl has taken up residence a decade ago. He and his fleet demanded my old lord leave. He did. I stayed and sang the new lord's tunes. He let me worship Saint Barr as long as I also honored Thor, his patron, and truth be told, young man, I had no qualms about heathenism. I learned so many lovely heathen songs, and if God punishes me for it, then he is not the god I wish to worship. My only quarrel is that the heathens call the island Bare-island, because it looks barren from afar. But it's named Barr-island, after my Saint Barr! But lad, don't just let me blather on."

"Well, it's rather nice to hear my tongue," Asgeir said. "My mother is from Ireland, but she was raised on Eigg, and so was I. So we're neighbors. Gaelic is my first tongue."

"Eigg? My neighbor!"

"I'll be returning there soon, after nine years of living in Norway. I'm on a voyage to Ireland with Ulf the Old soon."

Saints be praised—I would love to return home, as stormbound as our isles are—but by good Mannanán," he said, calling the name of an old heathen Irish god, "this late in the year? It's nearly the slaughter month! The winds turn erratic, the days shorten, the storms sent by wrathful Thor against cocky sailors."

"My auntie said I'll survive," Asgeir said while swallowing dry, "but the rest of the ship will visit Ran's realm."

The skald halted his strumming for a spell, as if struck by the hex himself, then went back to it. "Your auntie's a heathen witch, then?"

"Aye. She sees the urd of men. I don't know if she causes it or just knows it, but she sees it. I don't want to go."

"Aye," Odharnait said, "I have a stone in my throat thinking about it myself. I wouldn't brave the ocean due west this late in the year. West is where we go when we die. Sailing now is just asking to wreck. But I see a twinkle in your eye, lad. I think you'll be just fine. Just keep your wits about you, and always stay loyal to your gods, even if they be heathen."

"Thank you, neighbor."

"Now off with you—drink and be merry, who knows how long any of us will walk this mortal rock!"

He hummed low as he picked the strings, and he raised his voice. Two young lasses in linen dresses danced about now, kicking their heels as Odharnait strummed faster. In rhythm, they clacked their feet and clapped as the line of sailors drank more gulps from the barrel of mead.

"Come hither!" Saga shouted at Asgeir, her long plait draped over her shoulder. "Come on, stop pussyfooting about. The girls will look even better once you drink some of this!"

The sailors all laughed around the barrel of mead. Asgeir went over, the aroma of honey nearly greater than smokiness of the fire.

"One of Ulf's lads. Another son, are you?" she asked him.

"Nay," he said.

"I'm Asgeir, son of the huskarl of the King of Lothlend."

The lady of the house stiffened her body and bowed her head. She had a handsome face with a broad jaw and a small nose. Her blond hair, in one long plait, swayed far down her back. "My honors then," she said. "Odin blood you are, just as my husband. Come, take a drink, will you?"

Saga leaned over, filled the horn, and handed it to Asgeir. The horn had been cold and the sweet mead warm.

"It's the finest mead from Northumbria, in Angleland," she said. "We honor Odin with every sip. Go on, enjoy it, few do before Jul."

Something glinted at Saga's neckline as she adjusted her coat. An odd-looking bronze brooch, circular with a ruby embedded in its center like an eye. She noticed him looking.

"It was taken off one of their books down in Frankrike, from the monks. Can't remember if one lost it or traded it to my husband," she said with a smile as Asgeir sipped the mead from the horn. "You're not a Christian, outraged by such a blasphemy—are you?"

"No, I worship our gods," he said. "Ullr and Odin have visited my dreams."

"Ah! The gods bestow luck and riches and love upon those such as you," she said. "What a gorgeous brooch you have—Ulf the Old's sailor."

A sailor passed him a soapstone cup of ale as more sailors lined up to have fills of mead. Asgeir stepped out of line as Saga busied to refill the cups.

He fingered Ulf's brooch. *By Thor, I suppose it's not the worst fate, being attached to his pack.*

Asgeir sat on a down cushion at the bench of the western wall. He hadn't sat in such a comfortable seat in a long while, since he had left his house. He leaned back against the warm wall, drowsy. His head still reeled from the blows from Gealbu, and from those boys back at Rikheim. *Must have drowned, what a shame.*

He sipped his mead in big gulps because he was thirsty. He leaned his head back, and someone sat next to him.

"You're downing that fast," Rolf said as he sipped his own.

"Yeah," Asgeir said as he took an even deeper drought.

"All that fuss about the Svear woman and the Thing—we haven't feasted properly since the battle," Rolf said and he lolled his head back. "What a fight that was, back at Rikheim! You missed it." From his satchel, he presented a hand's length of a broken spearshaft, pocked in chips and scratches. Two notches had been etched into it.

"That day, I killed two men."

"Your father proud?" Asgeir said as he drank again. "What's that circle?"

"I won a holmgang."

Asgeir nearly asked *against who?* But it was merry, and he didn't want to spoil Rolf's humor.

They both went silent for a spell, until Njall sat next to Asgeir, nearly bouncing on the cushion underneath him. His feet didn't touch the floor of the hall.

"Speaking of Rikheim—what the fuck happened to you? I told you to stay put!" Njall said slurred. "Why'd you run off and get captured?"

"A girl lured me away."

Njall laughed. "That's stupid. Real stupid. I was stupid too when I was your age. Full of stupidness."

Rolf nudged Asgeir while grinning. "The Irish girl."

"Yeah," Asgeir said. "She tricked me to get waylaid by Ketill's sons. But I saved her life."

"She has the looks of a highborn such as us. She's well-fed, not hunched from farmwork. Her hair is shiny. Good she owes you, huh?" Rolf asked with a laugh.

"Not like that," Asgeir said. "Not like that at all. She told me I can't even look at her naked unless I'm her husband. My father always told me that I should never force myself upon a woman, even a thrall."

"Why would you marry a she-thrall?" Rolf asked. Before Asgeir could answer, Njall spoke, leaning over his face. Asgeir hardly heard what he said as he ranted with slurred speech and many stutters.

"The old goat's been grazing," Rolf said with a too-hearty laugh.

"Do you have a girl?" he asked.

"I've had a few," Rolf said with a coy grin, "but my father wants me to wed a woman somewhere down south. In Hjaltland or Orkney. A woman, not a girl, someone highborn."

"Yeah?"

"Yeah. But truthfully, I want someone wilder. With a fiery urd. And I want to like her."

"A fiery urd," Asgeir said. "That reminds of Sakka. I really do miss her, but her parents hate me. And I don't know if she'll still be married to Arild. And Éabhín, she has a flame inside her too, but she's just a thrall."

A red-faced sailor from near the hearth called Rolf, and he left. They tossed something into coals and laughed when it went sparking.

"I'll tell you about women," Njall slapped the upper-arm of Asgeir. "Women are like ships," Njall said, but didn't continue his sentence.

Asgeir dozed, but flinched awake. He had slid down, and his chin poked the upright pin of his brooch to knock him out of his sleep. He adjusted it away from his face, leaned further back on his seat, and his eyelids closed. Then someone shouted in his ear.

"I'm talking to you!"

"I'm your first mate," Njall said, "and you disobeyed me. Where'd you go? Huh, where did you go? Off to see a girl? Do you know what girls some of your mates saw, while you were chasing after that girl like a fucking cat chasing a mouse?"

"Valkyries."

Asgeir stiffened awake, his cup caught upright in his tunic's skirt.

"Do you know how close I was to them?" Njall asked. "Where my friends are now? Where are they? Maybe they saw valkyries, maybe they didn't. One didn't. He shat himself and ran and caught a javelin in the back and died gurgling in the mud. Stupid.

"Odin the grim one, lord of wars, called us then. Could you imagine that? Look at Saga—look at her!"

Saga stood over the mead-barrel still, now ladling more into the soapstone cups of the sailors.

"What you say to that? Look how beautiful she is—like a valkyrie. The valkyries pour mead for the warriors in Valhalla. Do you know that?"

"Of course I do. I'm the son of Hallgeir Gael-Slayer."

"Imagine it. Odin calls you up to Valhalla, his beautiful valkyries pick you up and fly you there, and you get to look at 'em all you want!"

He rambled on about valkyries and Freya in Volkvangr. Odharnait strummed his lyre, and the light struck its amber bridge and glowed. The soapstone cauldron over the fire had been bubbling as men lined up for stew. The brooches of Saga shimmered when she twisted her body to the tune of the lyre, dancing, and Haakon uncloaked himself and apprehended her and they danced in front of the long-hearth. Asgeir's chin touched his chest.

Row after row of warriors stood in a great hall as wide and tall as the deepest, highest cavern back on Eigg. The walls had been painted with oxblood with fringes of azure, and the fire longer than a ship. The warriors all stood sworded and mailed, with iron helmets that gleamed smoothly like so many river rocks. They all sat on wooden, high-backed chairs at a table with a scarlet tablecloth with the finest ceramics and silver cups. Asgeir found himself among them, Gael-Kisser belted around his waist, where it belonged. Something furry touched his bare legs, and he found a dog down there, licking up some crumbs. *Beardy? Beardy, my old sheepdog? You died so long ago… I had only been nine winters when you passed.*

Asgeir knelt down and ran his hands all over the dog's neck.

At a barrel with gilded staves, three women stood over it. They all wore red-plumed helmets, and with two hands, they dipped the longest horns Asgeir had ever seen—aurochs horns—into the mead. They wore red cloaks and had stern faces, but they were so beautiful that Asgeir sat awed.

At the head of the table, a figure sat in a golden mail shirt, with a fur-lined purple cloak. He had a long gray beard that hung over his mail like beardmoss over a gold trunk. The old man had just one eye, nothing but a red gap for the other. Two wolves sat at each side of his armrest like guardians, silent but weary. Asgeir knew where this was, and he wept, for he was dead.

Odin in Valhalla.

He blinked a few times, and found himself in a wide, soft bed, with the comfiest pink pillows under his head. Next to him, a woman with curly locks like firetongues that danced over her naked, white body as she twirled in the bed. The Gaelic girl? He embraced her.

"I died in battle, but my sword is by my side. I earned Valhalla."

"I don't want you in Valhalla, I want you here with me," Éabhín said in Gaelic.

"Why am I here? I want to go back and see the valkyries…"

Éabhín brushed the hair from her face, and she smiled and in a honeyed voice said, "you haven't earned it yet."

Now the ocean stretched in endless gray. The bed was nothing but the sea, formless but cresting. He floated there, and the voice of his heckling aunt thrashed about. "To Ran!"

Asgeir's dry mouth writhed, for he had seen Odin. *Oh, Auntie! If only you were here to explain my dream… did I really just see Odin in Valhalla? Will I die now? Why was Éabhín there? She was far less prickly than in this world. Maybe I should pay more mind to that lass.*

He awakened, blinked the bleariness from his eyes, and found a girl much alike to Éabhín. She wore a heavy, dark dress that contrasted against her white ankles and hands. She had thick red hair in a plait, unlike Éabhín's loose hair. She dipped about, twirling a finger through a strand, as she spoke to two taller lads in green tunics. Is that Éabhín?

Asgeir started toward her, and with a smile on her face, her eyes met his. She turned back to the two lads, but Haakon himself had gotten up and strode across the room.

"You're supposed to be on watch duty! Both of you!" Haakon shouted. The two lads stood frozen for a moment, then scrambled out the door, cold drifting into the longhouse as they did. The redheaded girl vanished with them. *Was that Éabhín? If it was, just what was she doing there with those two lads?*

The skald ceased his strumming as the guests all turned to the north end of the hall.

Haakon returned to his place of honor. He sat throned, the high-seat of the house, at the north-end of the fire. His throne was a wooden chair, carved with ravening beasts and hidden faces amidst snaking arms and hooked beaks, and it stood higher than the others around it. Only those of Odin's blood could sit in such a seat. The Allfather birthed kings and all kings worshiped him, even the Christian kings of Angleland and Frankrike and Lombardia honored him as their foremost alderelder. He sired the highest blooded jarls on Midgard, too, and one such lorded over his mead-hall now. Horn in hand, open-palm displayed to his guests, Haakon addressed his guests as Saga stood at his side.

"Today, we have gathered to mark the passing of a horrid three days in our valley. Many men have died, many widows wail, and many orphaned children weep at the graves of their fathers. What have we to gain from this? We have nothing to gain, and all to lose. We call on Freyr that we be blessed by peace. We all drink from the same mead, and welcome our honored guest, Gealbu, the chief of the Finnmen from Finnsnes who have ventured so far south over the tundra and mountains to visit Laerdal and my mead-hall. Much misfortune has befallen them while here, and we only wish that when they return to Finnmark they remember our hospitality, and not the mistreatment they endured. Please, step forward."

Gealbu entered the hall, with a drum in his hand and a drumstick in the other. The patrons of the hall gasped, for the drum had markings painted on it of little men clad in snowshoes and armed with ski-poles backdropped against zigzag patterns in alder-bark paint.

Sakka's father! Maybe he's calmed down. Maybe he will listen, and we can work out something where Sakka and I could see each other again.

But the Finnman walked forward without one look at Asgeir. He wore a broad-shouldered hood over his head with braided ties that cinched it under his jaw. His baggy trousers and pointed reindeer-skin shoes marked him out as more northern than even the northernmost Norseman.

Gealbu took a breath and let out a high-pitched bellow as he banged his drum. His drumbeats filled the hall as he beat the drumskin while he waddled around. He yelped, yipped, and let out throaty-bellows. His eyes lolled as he screamed and drummed hard, his body shaking and shivering to the quickening drumbeat.

Saga beckoned Haakon. The jarl, flushed and reddened, pointed to some of his oathsmen seated on the benches. Two men, one brunette and the other blond, stood up and marched over to the Finnman.

Did he just cast a spell?

Before the oathsmen could seize Gealbu, he locked eyes with Asgeir and he yelped, his tongue wiggling like a hatchling as he rapped his drumskin with flickering movements of his wrist. Then the two oathsmen dragged out the Finnman from the hall, out the ingang and into the night.

Asgeir, confused, turned to the sailors, who all shook their heads. Ulf screwed up his face.

"That was aimed right at Asgeir," Njall said to Ulf. "Our journey has been cursed twice now."

"No need to fear the savage," Ulf said loudly as he marched back to the mead barrel and reached his hand out to Saga. "Let us keep drinking."

"Yes—forget that weird man," Saga said as she ladled more mead into the horn.

Jarl Haakon sighed and sat on his seat with his fist against his graying chin. "I must atone to you all for that."

The pair of thralls stirring at the cauldron over the hearth beckoned Saga over, and she announced dinner.

They had slaughtered a suckling pig earlier in the day, buried it in ground and covered it in heatstones. Then the thralls had fetched and prepared it. Saga brought it out on a platter, and when she placed it, Haakon sliced the tender meat from its legs as the skald sang a hymn to Freyr. The house-thralls served soup and flatbread to the guests along with ale.

Did Gealbu hex me? By Thor, I should ward myself from it! Poor lass—her father hexes me, yet she may carry my baby! His eyes darted about the hall. Ill-luck could mean death for him at the worst.

Just as Asgeir had the tenderest-looking pork slathered on his plate, a voice shouted from outside the hall, and someone rushed in. He was a young man, sweaty with a tight green tunic, one of the watchmen who had been slacking off with that redheaded girl.

"We're under attack!"

Haakon threw his cloak over his shoulder and unsheathed his sword in one swing.

"Who dares tread upon my feast?"

"I don't know—but there are two ships rowing up the river, and they shot arrows at our watchmen!"

"Two ships?" Haakon looked at his armsmen. Asgeir reckoned he had thirty or so men. "Then we must flee up to the hillfort! Do we have time, man?"

"If we make haste," the watchman said.

"We leave double-quick, all of us!"

Haakon's men started forward for their weapons in a mass. Jarl Haakon took Ulf by his forearms.

"Ulf the Old—we are under assault by an unknown foe—will you fight by our side?"

Ulf threw his cloak back in the manner of Jarl Haakon. "We carve the eagle on the back of those that threaten our host! Could we look in the eyes of our fathers if we didn't? Sailors, to arms!"

With that, the oathsmen ripped the shields and spears off the walls of the mead-hall, and a torrent of men rushed outside— Asgeir among them— into the bitter-cold breeze under the full moon that lit the night.

Ulf led his oarsmen to the Sea-Bitch, which had been dragged up the riverside. The captain barked orders as his crew clambered up the planks and ladders, ransacking the ship, each chest yawned, each bag thrown open, each sailor grabbing a spear and shield. Asgeir awaited his weapons. He had seen Valhalla and Odin, and thought the hooded crow back at the moot had been the harbinger of it all, sparking it forward like a strike of steel on flint.

"Odin himself calls us to war!" Ulf said as sailors ran past. "We will give the ravens a feast tonight, and you won't get a morsel unless your worms eat your enemy in the ground!"

Asgeir knelt down to pet Svartganger, who sat shivering and round-eyed twixt two chests belowdecks. *May be the last time I see you, old friend.*

Njall tapped the deck behind him. He turned to find the small man with a one-handed spear and a shield. He tossed Asgeir one and then the other.

"You know how to use a spear?"

"Not really. Just a sword."

"Prick the pointy end in the enemy," Njall said, and moved on.

Asgeir turned the spearshaft in his hand, pushed the shield forward, and jabbed the air with an overhand grip. He hadn't ever been a spearman, rather a swordsman as his father and brother had taught him. But Ulf the Old carried his sword, and the other swords had been smithed for their specific wielders, so there was not much to do but to prick the enemy with the pointy end of the spear.

"Hurry the fuck up!" Ulf the Old shouted from the shore, his rows of spearmen all at the ready. Njall walked past the warriors, his own sword in his hand, counting heads. Asgeir ran off the ship with some other stragglers and lined up in the back row.

In the dark gloom of the distance, two ships with colorless sails rowed up the river. Ulf the Old unsheathed Gael-Kisser and struck through the air toward the ramparted hill. Asgeir and other sailors followed, half-drunk as they staggered up the breast-like, treeless hill.

Behind them, the ships scraped on land just below the hill. The enemy warriors hurried one-by-one down the planks of their drakkars. Asgeir stood gape-mouthed for a moment until Foul-Farter slapped his shield, snapping him out of it.

They continued up the steep hill. The trackway up was crowded with men, so that Asgeir and some others ran up the hillside, weaving through trunks and large stones. They arrived at the first wall, where a dozen of Jarl Haakon's bowmen waited.

They all rallied around Jarl Haakon, who waited on the flat top of the hill. Haakon and Ulf conversed up there as the enemy approached the bottom of the hill, shadows dancing about the darkened land like hand-puppets against a firelit wall. They swung toward the west around the base of the hill, and the bowmen loosened their bowstrings.

Iron-tipped arrows zipped down the hillside. Asgeir didn't know if they had sent enemies writhing into the ground, but other men trudged up, shields over their heads, turtle-like, as the bowmen loosened another volley of arrows into them.

Some men groaned and others fell. One man stood there, an arrow in his torso, holding onto it as he retreated. Other arrows flew into the black yonder. Their foes kept trudging up the hill, shields-at-the-ready. A banner fluttered above them, and in the moonlight, Asgeir saw it had been a red tattered cloak caught in the wind.

Ketill Redcloak's torn cloak! It must be his men out for revenge!

Njall ran down the hill. "Come on," he said, starting away from them, "follow me now, get your weapons, we're going to earn our salted cod. Erle— you're in command!"

The sailors all ran along the hill, leaping around brambles, stumps, and rounded boulders. Asgeir followed them, and there, they found a horde of men moving up the hill, some with arrows stuck out of their shields like hedgehog spines, frayed goosefeathers ruffling in the breeze.

"Form up!" Erle said, and Asgeir hadn't known what he meant.

The sailors all melded into a wedge-like formation, the youngest in the front. Foul-Farter grabbed Asgeir and hauled him forward, and he stood now at the center of the formation.

"Shield up, follow what Erle says," Foul-Farter said. "Stab them when they come close—and for fucking Helvete—keep your shield up and stay alive!"

The slope screamed with men, and the hot breath and musk of them all engulfed him, and he found himself carried away much like the nails on his shield nailed his boss to the planks.

He thrust his spear wildly, without target, against the line of enemies. The foremost among them wore red cloaks. *Ketill Redcloak's kin?* The wedge of men drove into them, and they all crashed hard like hammer on wood.

Asgeir stabbed with his spear, first at an alarmed youth younger than he, then against a lean man with a broad shield, until an enemy spearpoint checked against his shield, and a jolt went through his left arm. *One misstep and I am dead.*

"Come back!" Erle shouted. Asgeir found himself backing up the hill, stumbling but righting himself on a stump, until he had put some distance between himself and the enemy.

Their foes hadn't perused, but a commander behind their line shouted "hold!" and then "throw!", and they cast their javelins at the sailors.

Javelins whizzed through the sky, whistling about. One sailor moaned and crashed down the hill. Asgeir felt one punch through his shield; the point rasped his shin.

"Raise your shield higher, you fucking idiot," Erle said to him. He complied, and more javelins landed around him, plunging into the ground. One juddered from a tree stump next to his leg, and he found himself falling backward over the first low stone wall of the rampart.

The enemy came forward, despite hissing arrows and soaring javelins in their direction. Their banner, a red cloak, still stained the sky like a splash of blood on the ground after a slaughter.

"Get that banner!" Erle shouted. "Rip it off from the fucking pole!"

Ulf put one foot on the low wall and aimed a javelin toward the waving flag below.

"Are you cowards?" he asked, "is the crew of the Sea-Bitch as meek as little girls? Onward and let us feast guiltless tonight!"

He lunged over the wall and started toward the banner-lord. The sailors cried out as they ran across the hill. Asgeir had gotten caught up with them and raced toward it.

The javelins had quieted, the arrows had ceased, for the enemy lined up in a shieldwall and spearwall and iron met wood until the ground was soaked in rivulets of blood.

A row of warriors came forward, spears jutting like the prongs of a weft-beater, alight with moonbeams. Ulf's sailors edged forward, and the two sides stopped just out of spear's reach.

Shields went up on all sides. Iron scratched and scraped as both spearwalls held their spears aimed at the enemy, but no one dared to stab. A gap had formed between the two sides, though Ulf's sailors still held the higher ground.

"What are you waiting for?" Ulf yelled as he elbowed his way right into the center of the line. "What stops you? Are you all cowards? What have you between your thighs? Balls or twats?"

Whether he spoke to his own men or the enemy, as soon as he uttered the last word, spears stabbed across the gap, banged against shields and bounced off each other's ash-poles. Thumps and rasps and hisses sounded as spearman vied against spearman.

Asgeir stood abreast with men taller than him, Foul-Farter to his left and Erle to his right. Long steel spearpoints thudded against his shield; his heart beat in rhythm with it. Gealbu's drum echoed in his mind.

"Watch that leg," Erle said as a spearpoint whisked over Asgeir's left thigh. He winced and jumped out of the line, but someone shoved him back into it.

"Asgeir! Watch that fucking leg!"

Asgeir thrust his shield downward, and a spear tip thudded against its rawhide rim. He found himself backing up, for all the line had backed up, and the banner-lord led some men up on their left flank.

They were pushed back five or six man-lengths, and someone shouted that they must fall back over the wall. Asgeir banged a heel on the knee-high stones, but no pain came. They all scrambled over it.

"Hold it here!" Erle shouted.

Asgeir held steadfast, but the thuds of steel against shields checked him. *So many spears…*

He jumped out of the line to let the spearpoints slide away. As he did, a spearpoint shoved into the right flank of Erle through the gap he had left. The sailor cried out as he crumpled out of the line, his shield over his face.

Fuck! No! Our commander!

Asgeir stepped back in line as the ranks closed over Erle's shivering body.

"Erle?" Asgeir cried down.

"He's dead—forget it!" the sailor that took his place shouted.

The enemy line had found equal footing now, but they could not move forward with the wall in the way. Both sides stopped for a spell, then a longspear appeared between two shielded men.

Pox on it all—someone's dead because of me! Maybe we'll lose, because of my carelessness…

"Two-handed spear! Two-handed spear in the center!" someone else shouted.

A tall, hatless man held a spear nearly the length of three men, with a thick blade large enough to slay a horse. He held it point upward across from Asgeir. Asgeir shirked away from the wall, but someone again shouldered him forward. The longspear came for him.

The blade crashed through his shield and splintered it asunder. The spear tip scratched the silver of his brooch as it sunk into his chest right through the eyelet, and pierced his cloak, tunic, and flesh. It felt hot, burning hot iron on the cold day. Asgeir stumbled out of the line, and he nearly fainted.

Someone held him up. "Useless as a lead sail," Ulf muttered in an undertone. "Who trained you?!" he shouted, and he spun with Asgeir, tossing him aside and out of the line and onto the cold grass. Njall whistled from the side as he pointed to Asgeir.

Asgeir lay there on the ground for a while, soaked in sweat and blood pooled underneath his tunic. A clawing pain crawled through his chest, and he bit hard into his own lip. *Someone died because of me… and maybe I'm going to die here.*

He still clasped his spearshaft, but the splintered shield lay somewhere else. The din of steel rang out as the two sides fought on either side of the wall. A he-thrall of Haakon kneeled over and lifted him up on his shoulders, and the spearshaft rolled out of his hand.

The thrall hiked up the hill with him until they reached the very top, where some women waited armed with needles and spiderweb. He found himself spun in the air and, when he hung there, he saw the red-cloak banner bearer: an eye-patched Arild, with a company of spear-armed Finnmen, known by their red-yellow tunics and hoods, which struck at the flank of the sailors.

Up on the hilltop, Saga approached him in a bloodied smock. The thrall laid him out and pulled his tunic off.

"It will be well, brave warrior," Saga said as she leaned over. "The goddess Eir is here to heal you." He stiffened his legs and yelped when the needle slid into him. Saga stuffed the hem of his own tunic in his mouth. He bit down, stars flashed before his eyes, and hot blood pooled out around his chest.

"The wound—it's not so bad," she said, "you will not die from it. Pray to Eir that no fester comes to you."

A bronze needle sank into him, and she hummed as she sewed. Asgeir couldn't see her for his tunic covered his eyes. She sang:

> *Spider's silk is worthy of scorn,*
>
> *In ugly webs the corners are adorned,*
>
> *Yet the stickiest web overgrown,*

By bronze and spiderweb your wound is sewn.

Eir our goddess heals the sick,

More than the dog can lick.

Eir, Eir, hear me high and low,

Guide by your hand this wound I sew

The burning needle wove in and out of him as she sang, his screams muffled by the tunic. She righted his garment from his quivering head, and gentle lips kissed his creased forehead. He had been gnawing at his tunic with spittle and breaths that pulsed out of his mouth. She stood and left him to hurry over to another wounded man carried to the top by a thrall.

I can't believe I was so stupid to step out of the line, and then to keep my shield so close to my body! Erle, I did you wrong...

Asgeir thrust himself to sit upon a wall to watch the battle rage below. Shields and spears thudded against the other. High above, a crow cawed and more crows cawed back from the forest like chanters, and soon dozens of crows flocked toward the hill, wheeling in the wind.

The great line of defenders had bowed. Haakon's men had been driven up from the first course of rampart and were now behind the second wall, lower with more jagged boulders, while the sailors fastened themselves at the first course. A dead enemy tumbled down from them as Ulf, his mail silvery in the moonlight, shouted "three!" loud.

Ulf backed out of the line and, after some barking, four men came with him. They dropped their spears and unsheathed swords. In an eyeblink they slipped past their comrades and smashed into the enemy line right at its thinnest. They broke through, swords slashing toward the banner-bearer. A horn blew from further downhill as the row of Haakon's men rushed the enemy and sent them fleeing. One retreating enemy got snagged by brambles and a sailor chucked a javelin; it impaled him, while other enemies fell to their knees with their weaponless hands on the ground.

Haakon's men began to shout, and the jarl himself dragged Arild by the collar of his tunic up the hill. His defeated foe bumped his head against the first course, he whimpered as his body slid over jagged rocks up to the second course. Haakon's men and the sailors gathered, some with enemy spears, or hands, their wounded and dying enemies piled into a heap of blood, gore, and moans. Together, they herded disarmed enemies, some bloodied, into a cluster.

At the third course, Asgeir saw Arild with a gash in his arm, wrapped up in a tattered red cloak. Haakon set Arild up on the third wall. Asgeir crawled closer down the hill, each handful of grass a new stab of pain. He propped himself up against a boulder so that he could watch, for many men had clustered about and clouded his vantage point.

"Take me hostage, please, my jarl! My mother will pay much silver for me. She begged me not to go!"

The jarl leaned his head skyward. "So Frida knew of this, too," he said. "Maker of chaos, what say you?" Arild had fallen to his knees, his eyes half-open, heaving. "Tell me, what was the purpose of this?"

"I'll tell you the truth, since that is all I have now. The purpose was to draw you out. Force you to surrender. If we won, we would have outlawed you. My father would sit at the jarl's seat instead of you. That's why we didn't attack you in the hall—it would have been my father's."

"And why would you?"

"You wronged us when you sided with that Asgeir and that Ulf. And lots of kinfolk were sore about it. That's why they attacked with us—and the Finnmen, who hate Asgeir."

I suppose I'll never get Sakka now… but I am pleased to watch Arild squirm.

"You settled your dispute with Asgeir through the duel. You lost, but came out lucky with just a wound. Yet you try your luck still? Did you not hear that crow? Asgeir! Come here!"

Asgeir struggled to stand up, his feet slipping on the muddy ground underfoot. Two of Ulf's men hauled him up and helped him limp down to Haakon and Arild. He stifled his whimpers as each step. The crowd had ringed them in a dense throng.

"It's clear as a rooster's caw that Odin himself has sent us a sign. Arild should have died after he lost his duel. Now our valley is blotted in red. To the crows with that!" Haakon said as Asgeir found himself close to the two men.

Arild writhed on the ground, unkempt in his tattered cloak, the stink of shit and blood about him. With a foot on Arild's back, Haakon nudged the huntsman forward. The jarl unsheathed his sword and awkwardly slapped the grip into Asgeir's trembling hands. The two sailors who supported him stepped back and left him unbalanced on his unsteady feet.

The hunter gazed up, his jaw jutted, his hood bunched up around his neck. Asgeir's straining eyes met Arild's single glassy eye while blood seeped down from his own chest wound.

Haakon seized Arild's hood and tore it off. His white neck appeared like the only unmarred part of him.

"To Odin we will sacrifice this enemy," Haakon said. "That is what I, the jarl and offspring of a jarl whelped by Odin when he was guised as Rig, know. Asgeir, I command you— in Odin's name— to behead this traitor, so we may please the All-Father with righteous bloodletting."

Asgeir sucked in a hard breath.

Me? Behead him? My father would die of shame if he saw me behead a cowering, kneeling man.

"Jarl Haakon," Asgeir said, "I can't kill a sitting man."

"Odin demands it."

"Allow me to kill Arild like a man, in a duel. It's what my father would choose."

"Yes," Arild said, "yes! That is right—let us duel again—to the death this time!"

"You're gravely injured," Haakon said as he glanced at the sewed-up bloody hole on Asgeir's chest. "And Odin has spoken."

Arild's misdeeds flashed before Asgeir's eyes: every single spiteful arrow that had shot his way, how he had barked at Sakka, when he had aimed his arrow down at defenseless Ulf in the pit, the noose he'd hung around Asgeir's neck, his lies to affront Tyr at the Thing, and his betrayal of Haakon.

He deserves to die, but still, not like this.

"As son of Hallgeir the Gael-Slayer, it's against my honor," Asgeir said, and lowered the sword.

"Yes—let us be honorable, Haakon," Arild said.

"Odin has spoken," the jarl said.

Asgeir stood thoughtless for a spell, and all withdrew from him. He found himself back in Odin's hall, the one-eyed god seated in his throne, his two quiet wolves at his knees. Asgeir found the one eye of Arild then, stark raving fear spangled in it.

Haakon stared at him. Asgeir nearly shirked away. His eyes met the throngs of men, both Haakon's and Ulf's, ringed around them.

"Odin has spoken," the jarl repeated.

Asgeir raised the sword and, in one swoop, it chopped through Arild's neck. Blood fountained from his headless neck as his head rolled across the sward, checked off a hewn stone block, and stopped, face up. The one lightless eye of Arild still burst in fear, like an afterglow. His other eye looked hollower and deeper, and Asgeir found himself, for an eyeblink, looking at the eye socket of Odin in his hall.

What have I done?

The sword fell from Asgeir's hand. Haakon grabbed it and raised it overhead.

"Odin," Haakon said with a snarl. "Asgeir killed Arild Rudolfsson in your name! The victory is yours! Frida's silver will be yours!"

One of Haakon's warriors took the head and hurled it up into the air, and all of the men of the hillfort shouted.

Then they placed Arild's head on the longspear with the red cloak. Haakon's men shouted loud at the sight.

"Head sways something dim," one armsman belted out.

"After the fight so bloody grim!" a spearman shouted.

"The thunder of steel," they both sang.

"To the lord of spears' peal!" many men sang back. Soon the men captured the night in song as they clashed their spearshafts against their shieldfaces.

The jarl walked down the hill to the heap of dead and dying men. "To the gibbet with the ones that survive the night. Odin owns them now."

Asgeir held his sewn-up wound, still huffing. The crows all cawed now almost as loud as the men sang and waved their spears around. Ulf and his sailors danced about, Gael-Kisser slashing to flick blood from its blade in little globs all over the rampart. Meanwhile, Haakon's men crowded Arild's body as they kicked it.

My honor. I feel it has slipped away from me. My first victory, but is it?

Who trained me? My father did, but was it well enough to stand in the shieldwall? It was not good enough. Erle died because of me, and I come from the battlefield seriously wounded. If I survive this, I'd best train better. But... I escaped death, just as foretold in my dream.

Asgeir sat and watched, unable to stand, as his father's bloodied sword sheathed into Ulf's scabbard, and the skald of Barr-island strummed his lyre to the tune of the song that rattled throughout the hillfort.

I can't bring myself to sing along with them.

The song of victory carried out loud into the night, drowning out the caw-song of the crows, who had grown bold enough to peck at the heap of the wounded and dying enemies. Odin had taken his own.

CHAPTER IX

The God of Peace

Flies swarmed around the blue faces of nine men impaled through the ass and out the mouth at the gibbet. They hung there on the terrace, shadowed by the mountain trolls. The troll and the she-troll and their baby all gazed on from by the waterfall with their stony glare in the dawning day, over the ruined farmstead of Rikheim.

Asgeir had been wounded but still lived. The spearpoint had only slid into his breastbone, and he had been bandaged, but it hurt whenever he moved. He also didn't know how long he would live, sewed up by the skilled hand of Saga or not. If his wound festered and he died, he too could finally return home, be it stiff and gray, and that comforted him.

Besides Erle, one sailor of the Sea-Bitch had died to a Finnman's arrow, and another succumbed to his wounds from a javelin. Ulf decided to take the bodies aboard to bring them to their homes.

The freemen of Laerdal had gathered about the gibbet on the blustery day. There, Jarl Haakon spoke on a dais, his warriors spear-armed. Men and women from the entire valley had gathered there to witness the jarl's speech.

Asgeir swallowed puke as the sight of the crow-pecked corpses in the low light.

I survive, if my wound doesn't take me. Thank you, Saga. By Thor—my first battle. To be called to defend my host's home—that was glory. If only I had been better at fighting, then I could share in the honor. I didn't know you well, Erle, but I will not let another man die because of my fear.

"To Odin with the criminal," Haakon said, "the vagrant, the traitor. No longer they besmirch my land with their lawlessness."

"Last night," the jarl continued, his eyelids baggy and black, "we learned of the traitor's plot. Arild, son of Rudolf High-Hat, gathered up some men who were faithless in my judgment, too cowardly to tell me to my face, along with his cousins and others; all spurred on by the promise of much silver from Orkney by Frida. Word has gotten to us that the wretch herself had fled already, but Arild weaseled away from her to join the fight—because he wished for Asgeir's head. He convened with the Finnmen to avenge the honor of their daughter. Gealbu's hex should have dampened our spirits, and though worried, we fought on, though not one Finnman was injured, and they escaped into the mountains unscathed. They deigned to draw us to the hillfort for their assault, for Frida wished to leave my hall Borgund intact, so that her husband could return and sit his treacherous ass on my seat. How they erred there, the fools! They could not take the second course, as the crew of the Sea-Bitch held the flank of the first course.

"Now, Arild's head," he said, as he opened the lid of a wicker box set with a severed head, and shimmied it upon the longspear that had once flown his banner.

Now Sakka is a would-be-widow. By Thor, I would take her as my wife now if I could. I won't mourn you, Arild, but rest. You fought bravely there in the end, as treacherous as that attack was.

Haakon leaned his foot against the spear-butt, which had been carved to a sharp point, and sank it into the ground. "May he have his eyes picked out by Odin's pets. Let it be known in this valley that I have slain the usurpers, and that Harald Finehair himself will hear about this and avenge us against Frida and her husband, that unruly jarl of Orkney, for he is bitter that the gods judged him and his wife an outlaw. He will deny that Odin himself judged his son, in the end, a sniveling coward. And he and his friends faced the hand of the Hanged One, in the form of my sword-hand." He raised his spear.

'When he scanned over the crowd of sailors, they raised their spears in salute back to Haakon. Asgeir raised his spear too, but a winch of pain stretched about him. He lifted his spear anyway.

"We thank Ulf the Old and his crew of brave sailors for their valor, and the victory we were granted today only came after much bloodshed. Lord

Freyr reminded us that if we wish for peace, we must carry a sharp sword, and the ground we prosper on must drink much blood.

"With that," he said and beckoned two of his men in red cloaks forward. They dragged a chest by a rope tied around it. Haakon opened the chest and a glimmer struck Asgeir's eyes. A trove of silver.

"This is plunder from our enemy that we won in battle, but we owe Odin this victory, and Odin shall receive his spoils."

The jarl's men took up bone-bladed shovels and parted the earth, digging until a long shaft had been carved out of the earth. Haakon lifted the chest in a heave and poured a stream of silver into the ground. Armrings. Rings. Ingots. Hacked-up slivers. Rods. The white metal poured in dings and chinks like the chariot of Måne, god of the moon, himself. The men all cheered as Haakon's men shoveled dirt over the treasure, until the glossy hoard turned matte and browned.

"Let any man who dares touch this treasure be hexed by the trolls that guard it," he said, pointing trollward.

"Tonight we sleep undisturbed," the jarl said. "And now," he approached Ulf and his sailors. With a smile he embraced Ulf the Old and, one-by-one, he embraced each of the sailors. When Haakon got to Asgeir he embraced him too, the jarl's scent a swelter of sweat and lilac. Asgeir cringed, for his spear-wound had scratched against his tunic, but Haakon had treated him just the same as any of the other sailors.

If only my father could see me now...

When Haakon had embraced the last sailor, he threw his cloak behind his shoulder and pointed westward. "For our thanks, we supply you with stockfish, tar, and sea-clothes for your journey to Hjaltland. Now, we ask that the crew of the Sea-Bitch never returns to Laerdal."

The sailors gasped and looked about, unsure, but Ulf spoke.

"You posted that Ketill scum at the rivermouth to collect a tax for you, and that was the first kindling of this mess. So who's at fault here?"

"I will not have an argument on this day in honor of Lord Freyr, so I ask that you listen to me, Ulf the Old. Leave with your crew, and let our dale heal."

"Your mind changed like the tides. We fought for you. We won the fight for you. I lost two sea-hardened men. But this is unsurprising. Men nowadays are often thankless.

Haakon took a slow breath at that last word. "We've said all we needed to say. Farewell. Perhaps, someday, we will be friends, but not any time soon."

"We're unwelcome—so be it. I've had enough of you flimsy jarls—I'm off to Ireland, where men still have honor, and rule by strength, not misrule by flabbiness. I pray that Harald sets you all straight."

He's right—we fought—and men died—to defend Haakon and his hall. What rot that I find myself agreeing so hard with Ulf. He has honor... this Jarl Haakon falls short of what a jarl should be.

"We've given you supplies, we've thanked you, we've shared our victory. Now allow us peace."

Ulf just showed him a toothy grin and mumbled to himself as he turned to his sailors.

"You heard him," he said. "Let's go, the lot of you."

"May Njordr, god of travelers, look after you," Haakon said as Ulf started into the ploughland. Ulf turned back to him.

"May Njordr inspire you not to tax travelers unjustly."

Ulf and Haakon glared at each other for a spell, and with that, Ulf started through the field.

Asgeir and the sailors all walked through the trackway that parted the field, down toward the burnt longhouse where just char and scrap-wood remained. Ulf spat toward it, and the sailors reached the riverside and followed it, it roaring from the night's rainfall. They reached their ship, dragged up on the riverside with the others.

Thank you for looking out for me, my friends, Asgeir said to the troll family as he boarded the ship.

The sailors unfurled the sail, some pushed the ship from land and then boarded, with the river current to carry them down to the fjord. They would reach the ocean before nightfall.

Asgeir found his rowing-place awaited him. That unremarkable stool with a wicker basket between its three legs seemed to greet him. It urged him on to sit down and row with the crew of the Sea-Bitch, on the lookout for honorable engagements. Off to Ireland where, along the way perhaps, he could regain his honor.

From his stool, Asgeir watched the farms go by as the ship left the Laerdal fjord.

The voyage is finally here. Late in the year, forewarned against by all sailors, doomed by my Auntie Bjorg. But she guaranteed my survival, and I'd believe her, if not for that Gealbu. My destiny, my urd, is tied to Ulf's, his warp to my weft. I've nearly been banished along with him now, and surely, I can never rest easy in Laerdal again.

If I ever return to Norway. It is fitting that Ulf heads southward, too. I will avenge Odd someday, and my sword will return to me. Once we get down there, I will find my father, and he will have the King of Lothlend right this injustice. Perhaps not even by duel…

"Something's troubling you," Ulf said as he paced from the keelson to the rudder. "Why so dour? We won, and a new adventure beckons us."

"I didn't want to kill Arild like that. I thought he should die in a duel. But Haakon refused."

Ulf grinned. "You bested him already in a duel. That was just a delayed ending."

"No," Asgeir said. "To behead a warrior like that, seated on the ground, when I had not put him in that state…my father would be ashamed. I feel that my honor is lost."

"Well then, nothing I say will bring your honor back. Nothing anyone says can. Only deeds can. Come on, lad, we sail the ocean today! Sail with me, fight alongside me, and since our crew is honorable, your honor will return to you."

"I've already fought alongside you and your crew, Ulf. I admit, I hated you since our holmgang, but if you can help me get my honor back, I will fight for you."

"Then fight for me, and get better at it. It seems we're the last ship of honorable men on Midgard, so fight for us and your honor will return," Ulf said.

"But don't think I won't find my father and make this all right, through law and through honor." "Very well then—now, row, sailors, row!"

The captain moved away amidships.

Asgeir turned his head up toward the steep-sided mountain to the east, and wondered where Sakka had gone. The Finnmen must have taken her when they fled, all the way back to Finnmark. He would never see her again, never feel her lithe body against his, her silky black hair soft against his face, her quaking body under his. And she had been an honest one, to testify against her future husband. The poor girl! To have her as a wife would have been a blessing from Freyja herself. And what a deal—even Harald himself kept a Finn wife, and they rewarded him with much reindeer antler for his comb-makers and walrus-hide ropes for the rigging of his fleet.

Svartganger jumped up onto his lap, and he petted the cat's head behind the ear as he purred.

"Moping about that girl, huh?" Rolf said as he wiped sweat from his thick brow, since he had rowed hard in the sunlight. "Too bad we couldn't catch the Finnmen, we could have gotten their girl for you."

Éabhín, who was still sewing up the spare sail, raised her red head up from the deck. "What, you going to do now, Asgeir, cry?" she asked in Gaelic.

He glared at her and her unbound hair. Before he could ask her if she had attended the feast in Haakon's hall, Rolf spoke.

"You were lucky, but unlucky yesterday. Can you keep rowing? I can vouch for you to my father if you can't."

"I can keep rowing," he said. "It hurts, but I'm just happy to be alive."

"To die in battle is not so bad," Rolf said, and he leaned heavenward. "There are worse ways to go than clung to a valkyrie. But I think you'll live. Your thread is just frayed, not severed."

"You're right," Vaage, a thick-bearded sailor, said as he munched on some dried cod, his legs apart on the deck as the ship dipped as it rounded a small ness. "That Saga is known for her skill with the needle. Asgeir here could have been far unluckier."

"It wasn't luck," Njall said, ducking under the rigging, "that Asgeir was stuck, or lack of it. He should have dodged that spear—he slacked off and let the spear hit him. A blade that big could impale a bull—hardly a shield on Midgard could withstand it."

"Why didn't you dodge it, man?" Rolf asked Asgeir.

"He's new to all of this—he'll do better next time," Njall said. "We'll train you more. Not much of a line fighter, are you?"

"I mostly learned to fight through duels. I never have been raiding or warring."

"It shows," Vaage said. "You stepped right out of the line and left it open. Hope you learned your lesson then."

"I'll never let anyone die because of me again," Asgeir said, and stroked the oar hard and sucked in his pain. Vaage spoke, but he spoke over him. "I'll fight as hard as my father."

Erle, I won't let your friends down again…

Ulf walked up to the prow and turned to his men to address them. Seagulls wheeled in the air and darted about the rigging of the ship. The planks creaked as the first surge of the ocean melded with the fjord-mouth.

"Today, we finally leave Norway, luck be with us! Tonight we sail for Hjaltland, and then to Orkney. Sailors! We will find plunder there, for we will raid Rudolf High-Hat, and bring that wretched wife of his to justice. May that cunt's body garnish our prow!"

Sakka, I'll see you again, if your father's curse leaves me unscathed.

The sailors all cheered loud, and there was much merrymaking aboard the Sea-Bitch as it finished its trek of the longest fjord of Norway and reached the Norvegr just before nightfall.

Asgeir caught the scent of flowers. Éabhín, with a bundle of tansy in a shoulder bag, plucked up a pair of scissors that had slid away from her across the slick deck.

"Did I see you at the feast?" he asked in Gaelic.

She stared back, nonplussed.

"It was you! You distracted those watchmen?"

Asgeir halted his strokes and sucked in hard.

"I'm no slave," she said back in Gaelic, and she stared into his eyes.

She loved her master. I suppose that was her revenge. What could I do? Should I tell Ulf? It's far too late; the battle is over, and Haakon pissed him off anyway.

"You could have gotten us killed."

"I loved Ketill like an uncle," she whispered, "because he knew I am not a slave."

They both went silent.

"If you'll nay tell, then I'll reward you in Ireland."

"Reward me?"

"Aye. Maybe even help find your father. I said, I am no slave."

"I suppose I won't say anything, but I don't trust you now."

"Then don't."

She smiled until something crackled overhead. The waves grew choppier. Land faded. Gannets and other seabirds flew westward, rasping the sea, while the ship followed their course. Gray sea. Gray sky. Gray birds. The ocean-river widened into an endless froth. Asgeir rowed, each stroke a wince of pain from his spear-wound.

Green lightning reached across the horizon like the many tines of an antler. A thunderclap boomed so hard that some of the sailors startled from their stools. Svartganger loped away as the wind brought rain sideways.

"Don't worry, Svartganger. Auntie Bjorg assured us. We're going to survive. I hope. Long enough for me to get my honor back."

The words of his aunt rang in his ears:

To Ran with your ship,

A hex from my lip,

The waves I shall lead,

In the gray great mead.

"We've been twice cursed, the völva and the Finnman," Vaage said to Njall.

"And our captain kept insulting the trolls," Njall said.

"Quit your whining," Ulf said, one hand on the rudder as he gestured westward. "Nothing but baseless superstition—we ride the storm!"

So the Sea-Bitch sailed westward, grayness darkened to blackness, against the storm, the wrath of Thor aflame in the haze of the horizon.

The Viking Gael will return in Book 2 of the Viking Gael Saga.

Please Review this Book!

If you enjoyed The Viking Gael Saga then please leave me a review. A simple "I liked it!" is sufficient, or even just a star-rating. This helps bring positive attention to the book and my work, so I really appreciate it!

SUBSCRIBE TO MY NEWSLETTER

Receive the first chapter of the second book in

THE VIKING GAEL series if you sign up with your e-mail address!

Exclusive content and author updates!

SCAN THE QR CODE BELOW &

ENTER E-MAIL ADDRESS TO SUBSCRIBE

www.oldworldheroism.com

HAG OF THE HILLS

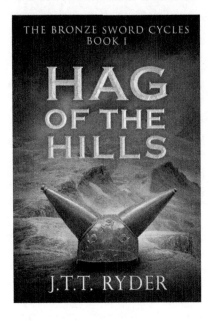

"Nothing is unconquerable; even our gods can die."

When the Hillmen murder his entire clan, Brennus is left no other choice but to live up to his family's legacy and seek retribution.

Now, he must survive endless hordes of invaders and magic-wielding sidhe, aided by a band of shifty mercenaries and an ancient bronze sword. Will he succeed?

Find out for yourself in "Hag of the Hills", the first instalment in the completed "Bronze Sword Cycles" historical fiction duology set in 200 B.C., steeped in Celtic mythology and culture.

http://books2read.com/hagofthehills:

THE LION OF SKYE

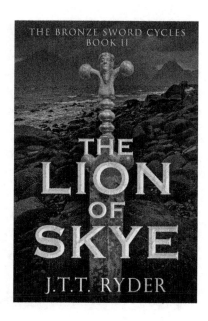

There can only be one Lion of Skye!

Vidav must defeat his brother in order to fulfil his oath to kill the Queen of the Hillmen.

If he does not fulfil his oath, his clan will be unavenged, and the Isle of Skye will remain under enemy rule.

If he does fulfil his oath, his brother may die.

Even worse, a dragon has been flying over Skye...

The Lion of Skye is the epic conclusion to the Bronze Sword Cycles duology, a historical fiction adventure set in 200 B.C. on the Isle of Skye, steeped in Celtic mythology and culture.

http://www.books2read.com/lionofskye

TOMB OF THE BLUE DEMONS

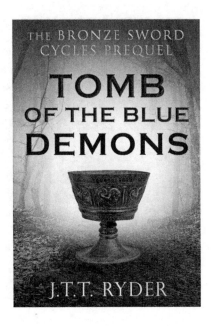

The Druid Ambicatos embarks on a journey of intrigue that quickly turns into war, when he arrives in war-torn Italia, under siege by the Carthaginians.

While the war rages, Ambicatos falls for a mysterious woman some call the Sorceress, who claims she has discovered the sight, the power of the Underworld.

Ambicatos must fight friend and foe alike in this epic novella, a prequel to Hag of the Hills, the Bronze Sword Cycles duology.

This novella is part of Celtic historical fiction series The Bronze Sword Cycles, set in 200 BC.

http://books2read.com/tombofthebluedemons

ABOUT THE AUTHOR

Joseph Thomas Thor Ryder is an archaeologist and author of the historical fiction. He is a published author of Viking archaeology, and a doctoral candidate specializing in the Viking Age and Celtic Iron Age. He resides in Norway where he conducts archaeological research and writes heroic fantasy set in historical periods.

APPENDIX

Afterword

I am an archaeologist of the Viking Age. That means that I study the past through material culture – what people physically left behind. This can be anything from a sword in a burial, to a series of house foundations, to a handful of coins, to some charred grain to radiocarbon date. The Viking Age is my area of expertise, but I am by no means incapable of faults. I attempted to be as historically accurate as possible. Unfortunately, the deeper you dig into the past, the deeper you realize that total historical accuracy is impossible. Napoleon Bonaparte (paraphrase) said that history is a series of fables agreed upon. It is actually a series of interpretations debated. Therefore, this story is my interpretation of how life may have been like in the Viking Age, around the mid-late 9th century AD. It is not the only interpretation, or even my only interpretation.

Dating and historiography

This story takes place in AD 870. This is right at the eve of the (traditional, not necessarily historical) unification of Norway, attested to in many later sources such as the Sagas. Regardless of the historicity of Harald Finehair, Norway was still likely divided up by a series of petty kingdoms and/or jarldoms. People from western Norway were likely colonizing the islands of Scotland, such as the Orkneys, Shetland, and the Hebrides, though archaeological evidence is much stronger for Viking presence in the subsequent 10th century. Nevertheless, Viking incursions likely led to the unification of the Picts and Scots and the cultural disappearance of the former. The Faroes would have been colonized, and Iceland was discovered but (probably) not yet colonized. Dublin and other areas of Ireland were under control by the Norse, where proto-urban trade towns flourished, and Norse, along with Hiberno-Norse peoples, would have a presence around the island for the next several hundred years until the Norman conquest. To the south, the Danes were very much busy in England, but this series will not concern the Danelaw or Jorvik. At least, not yet.

Names

This book is a work of fiction, but takes place in what is now Norway. All of the placenames mentioned in the book are real places – some of them have been Anglicized. Personal names were chosen from a pool of Old Norse names attested to in the sagas, historical literature, and runestones, but also (mostly) Anglicized, or younger versions of older names were chosen to make the names more palatable to modern audiences (Rudolf, and not Hrudolfr, the Old Norse root).

Placenames

Angleland – England

Avaldsnes – historical and archaeological seat of a powerful Viking and Medieval king, in present day Karmøy, Norway.

Bjorgkum – Bjørgkum, a site of a summer market in Lærdal.

Damsgaard – Damsård – in modern Norwegian, nearby Bergen.

Dubh Linn – the Old Irish name for Dublin – Black Pool.

Frankrike – "Frank realm" – France.

Hjaltland – modern Shetland.

Karmoy – Karmøy, Norway.

Irland – Ireland.

Laerdal – Lærdal in modern Norwegian, located in Sogn og Fjordane.
Lombardia – Lombardy in modern Italy.

Norvegr – a name attested to for Norway, likely designating the sea-route, but this is somewhat contested.

Norway – roughly what is now modern Norway. The word Norway may come from Norvegr – "the northern way", which would be the sea-route along the western coast of Norway.

Pictland & Skottland – modern day Scotland

South Isles, the – The Hebrides

Historical figures

Harald Finehair (850 – 932) – traditionally known as the first King of Norway, who unified the petty kingdoms and jarldoms of Norway as well as Norse-colonized islands of Scotland. His historicity is disputed; but I like to think he existed.

King of Lothlend, the – Lothlend, or Laithlinn, is a kingdom mentioned in the Irish Annals, contemporary with our period. Likely, it designated some political union of Vikings from Norway. Just where this kingdom was located has been disputed by scholars for decades. For this series, I located it in the South Isles (Hebrides), where I personally believe it was located.